KNIGHT'S LEGION MC

AVENGING
ANGEL

NAOMI PORTER

Copyright © 2021 by Naomi Porter

Naomi Porter/Ocean Dreams Publishing

www.naomiporter.com

www.oceandreamspublishing.com

Publisher's Note: This is a work of fiction. Names, characters, places, and incidents are a product of the author's imagination. Locales and public names are sometimes used for atmospheric purposes. Any resemblance to actual people, living or dead, or to businesses, companies, events, institutions, or locales is completely coincidental.

Book Layout and Cover Art ©2021 Cat at TRC Designs

Ordering Information:

Quantity sales. Special discounts are available on quantity purchases by corporations, associations, and others. For details, contact the "Special Sales Department" at the address above.

Avenging Angel/ Naomi Porter -- 1st ed.

ISBN: 978-1-952423-30-7

KNIGHT'S LEGION MC

AVENGING
ANGEL

CHAPTER ONE

MADELINE

I sang the last notes of my song and curtsied before the crowd of bikers, old ladies, and kittens feeling on top of the world. Storm's brothers cheered and clapped. Probably because they were drunk off their asses—not because I was that good, but I appreciated their enthusiasm. Hell, I ate up the attention. Adrenaline pumped in my veins. I couldn't stop smiling.

Fanning my face, the air appeared thicker—a sure sign of rain. The twilight sky was full of dark clouds rolling in from the west. It wouldn't be long, maybe an hour, before it drenched everyone. Not the best conditions for an outdoor orgy tonight. My mind went to a funny picture of those rough and tumble bikers going at it in a thunderstorm.

The humidity would make my hair frizzy and my skin sticky. But it didn't matter. I felt marvelous after singing for my new family and *my* man.

The she-devil caught my eye. I imagined she hated me even more after seeing me sing—no sweat off my brow. Carla could kiss my ivory ass for all I cared. There was a new queen in town.

After tonight, Carla was G-O-N-E, gone.

I looked over at my guy, expecting him to be grinning after getting his way. Or striding straight up to the stage to carry me off to bed where he'd lavish me with kisses and praise. Blow my mind with his talented tongue and fuck me into tomorrow. I expected to be spoiled.

But he wasn't even looking at me. It hurt my ego a little. Though I wouldn't let it show or act like a spoiled diva. That wasn't me. But not having Storm's eyes on me at this moment cut me more than it should. Why wasn't he looking at me?

I followed his line of vision across the lawn. *What is he looking at?* It wasn't a what, but a who. I gasped, placing my hand on my chest. Were my eyes deceiving me? I blinked several times. This must've been a dream or the effects of the whiskey screwing with my vision.

It was neither.

Toby, my brother, was on the Knight's Legion compound.

How did he find me? I hadn't mentioned Storm to my family.

My brother stared back with a stunned expression. Neither of us moved.

I turned toward Storm. He appeared shell-shocked. Like the Reaper he offhandedly mentioned from time to time was coming for him… or me. I saw his Adam's apple bobbing up and down. His eyes were wide, mouth agape. Sugar shook his arm, but he didn't acknowledge her.

What was going on?

Was he upset that Toby somehow breached compound security? Storm was very careful to approve the party guest list.

My eyes flitted toward my brother, then back to Storm. Back and forth, my gaze ping-ponged like I was watching a tennis match. It wasn't the look I expected playing on their face. No, it was more familiar. Like they knew each other. But how could they?

Everyone faded around me as a sense of doom settled in my veins. All I heard was the violent thumping of my pulse in my ears. What was I missing? What was between my brother and the man I loved?

Toby. Storm. Toby. Storm.

I locked eyes with my man. *Tell me what's wrong, baby... how do you know my brother?*

We stared at each other as if waiting for the other to make a move. My feet couldn't budge, like this moment took all my power from me. I wanted Storm to take me into his arms. To hold me protectively. Whatever was happening made me cold and clammy. So cold.

I needed warmth. I needed *his* warmth. I needed *him* to save me. *Come to me, Kaleb.*

Storm's cousins, Maddox and Markey's, laughter registered in my ears. All at once, it hit me. The familiarity I'd felt with Storm became clear. The fog lifted. My eyes were open. The feeling of knowing him in another life wasn't some weird déjà vu.

I had known him...

My childhood flew through my mind at supersonic speed, transporting me to Lake Waleska. I had spent the best week of my life with my family and KC, my brother's best friend.

KC's dad was the president of the motorcycle club in Garrison. I was so young. I never knew much about the bikers. My parents had sheltered me as much as they could. Toby and KC always redirected my questions. Eventually, I forgot about KC's dad being a biker. Then KC left town after Tommy died and never came back home.

Only KC was his nickname....

Blood drained from my limbs, pooling in my gut like a bad pot of chili.

Knight's Legion.

Knight.

Kaleb.

Kaleb Knight.

My heart felt like it jumped into my throat, choking me. All this time, Storm was Kaleb, the teenage boy I'd loved since I was a little girl.

Tremors rolled through my body. My head spun, hands slick with sweat. The mic slipped from my hand onto the wooden floor, clanging in the speakers. I wobbled down the stairs.

With my stomach doing somersaults, I managed to run to Toby. He lifted me into his arms.

"What are you doing here?" I cried, needing to hear my brother confirm my suspicions.

"I'm... I'm here to see..." He set me on my feet and gripped my shoulders. "What are you doing here, Maddy?"

"I'm here... I... I'm with..." I stuttered, the words lodged in my throat.

"Spit it out, Maddy!" His wild blue eyes searched mine.

"I'm with... Storm." His road name came out instead of his birth name as a panicked shudder ripped through me. I knew in my heart it was him. My love from the past.

Toby's eyes bugged out. "You're with Storm? How did you and Kaleb get together? When? Why didn't you tell me? Jesus Christ, Maddy, this is insane." He ran his fingers through his dark brown hair, avoiding my gaze. I recognized this look. He wore the same ill expression for years after Tommy's death. I never questioned why, assuming he had taken his time with our brother for granted as I did.

I shook my head. My mind whirled out of control. Loud music played. People were lost in their own little world, not paying attention to my inner destruction.

I glanced at Storm's table. He was gone.

"Where's Storm?" I pulled away from Toby and turned in a circle. He wasn't in sight. Neither was Sugar. I scanned the yard, my heart hammering in my chest as I searched for my man.

Toby grabbed my shoulders, laboring to breathe. "Talk to me, Maddy." He appeared as confused and shocked as I was.

"I can't right now. I need to find Storm." I ran to the table. Toby called after me, but I ignored him. Justin stood nearby, but that was it. Where was everyone?

"Justin! Where did Storm go?"

The grim expression on his face nearly made my heart stop. He pursed his lips. "Storm took off on his bike. I don't know what happened. He just… left."

I whirled around and caught sight of Track talking to his dad, Raul.

"Track! Track!" I yelled, running toward him. I must've looked like a crazy woman because he was on his feet by the time I reached him.

He bent at the knees, getting eye-level—like I did with my students. "Are you okay? What happened?"

I realized I was crying. Tears rained down my face that I hadn't even noticed. "Storm's gone. Justin said he took off on his bike. You have to find him. He's not okay!"

Track capped my shoulder. "Calm down, babe. Why are you crying? You two have a fight or something?"

"Track!" Sugar ran up, gasping for air.

"Maddy, I need to talk to you. Right now." Toby grabbed my arm like he was freaking the crap out. Sweat dripped down the sides of his face. His blue depths were wild so unlike him. He was usually calm and collected, Mr. Professional. This unhinged side of him amped up my panicked state.

"Hey, man. Take your hand off her." Track pushed me behind him and got in Toby's face. Ready to protect me. No, ready to defend Storm's old lady. "Who the fuck are you?"

"Hold on." I put my hand on Track's arm to defuse the situation as other bikers started to take notice. "This is my brother, Toby. Toby Hamilton."

Track cut his gaze to mine, staring for a long second. I could almost see the wheels turning in his head as he pieced it together. "Your brother? Hamilton is your last name?"

"Oh, Jesus." Sugar put her arm around my shoulders. "Now, I understand why Storm took off."

Thunder rumbled off in the distance as I bobbed my head. "Yes. You have to find him."

"Well, fuck." Track ran his hand through his hair. "Fuck!" He roared louder than the next wave of thunder. "Why didn't you tell him who you were? He has to be flipping the fuck out. How could you deceive him like that?"

"Jesus Christ," Raul muttered.

"Track, stop," Sugar snapped. "She did nothing of the sort."

More tears streamed down my face. "I didn't deceive him. He never told me his last name, either." I was shaking so much, my legs may give out. "I just pieced it together when I saw my brother."

"You need to go after him," Sugar told Track, tucking me into her side as I broke into a sob.

Storm wasn't okay. It was as if I felt his pain. He needed me to keep him from breaking. I had to save him from falling off the edge.

"Goddammit," Track shouted. "Lynx! AJ!"

"What's going on?" Tara grabbed my hand, but I ignored her. A crowd formed around us. The hum of whispers competed with the sounds of the building storm. I felt utterly exposed and vulnerable without my man beside me, assuring me everything would be okay. I knew it wasn't okay, couldn't be further from it. I'd already lost Kaleb once. The thought of losing him again made me weak at the knees. My head buried deeper into Sugar's shoulder.

"We'll find him." Track lifted my chin, getting my attention. "We'll find him, but I warn you, he may not want to talk to you."

"Don't tell her that," Sugar hissed.

"Hey babe, what happened?" Lynx appeared in front of me. "Why're you crying?"

"I'll fill you in. Let's go!" Track stalked off with AJ hot on his heels.

"Yeah, okay." Lynx followed but kept looking back with concern in his eyes.

"You conniving bitch!" Carla seethed. "He'll never forgive you for this."

"Back the fuck up, slut." Tara stepped between Carla and me. They started arguing, but I tuned them out.

I didn't know what to do. My life was spinning out of control. KC was Storm? The shock lingered in my mind, thoughts spinning on repeat. How could Kaleb leave me? What was I supposed to do now?

Toby jerked me out of Sugar's arms and tugged me away by the hand. My world was falling apart in front of dozens of people. Only a few seemed to notice. The rest were either too drunk to care or were screwing. I prayed the club wouldn't hear what happened by morning. Hell, I hardly knew what happened.

But it wasn't about me. Storm was the club's president. If he didn't come back, they would all be devastated, and it would all be because of me.

Toby took me inside the clubhouse and put me in a chair. I completely broke down as he held me.

"Just let it all out." Sugar had followed us and was sitting beside me.

I felt numb, like I was going into shock. Kaleb Knight was Storm, the president of Knight's Legion. It was right there the whole time. How did I not figure it out sooner? Guilt swirled in my body like the energy couldn't find anywhere to go. Of course I didn't recognize him. He looked nothing like the teenager I'd loved.

I didn't look the same either. KC had left right after Tommy's funeral. That was the last I'd seen or heard from him. I was only eleven. A twig with braces, and totally forgettable.

A painful breath emerged from my lips as I reached for a napkin to wipe my tears. I shook my head in total disbelief. Every moment with KC filled my head like my brain couldn't decide which one to focus on. I remembered KC as a tall, pretty boy with a trim, athletic build. A smooth baby face. KC was the sweetest guy in the world with the most unusual gray eyes. They changed colors with his mood. When he was angry, they darkened like a thunderstorm rolled in. When he was happy, they shimmered like platinum. I hadn't seen eyes like his until Storm's.

Shit, shit, shit!

I should've seen the similarities. But KC had dramatically changed. His overall appearance was nothing like the teenager who stole my heart. Storm had corded muscles, tattoos, a black beard, and rings on his massive hands. He was dark and dangerous.

My man was sexy and sinful. Short-fused. Controlling. He made me feel adored and loved when we were together.

In the last twelve years, we'd both changed. KC had become Storm, and I was no longer a twig with braces.

How did I not see the resemblance? Why didn't I question him after sensing I'd known him in another life? *Stupid.* I had known him in another life! He was my childhood crush, the boy I'd loved. Even after all these years, Kaleb Knight still owned my heart. I'd fallen in love with him all over again, only the adult version this time.

Oh, my God. I had sex with Kaleb Knight. Lots of dirty, sinfully delicious sex.

My face heated, probably turning red. It was stupid, but I felt so embarrassed. The things Kaleb did to me and I did to him; mercy...

"You need to tell me how this all happened, Maddy. I'm pretty damn confused right now." Toby rubbed my back.

"Well shit, Toby. Can't you see she's shell-shocked? Give her a minute to process," Tara told him in a scolding tone. She must have followed us into the clubhouse, too. I was so out of it I hadn't noticed.

Toby let out a frustrated huff. "I don't understand how this happened."

"What's there to understand? They met. They hooked up. They're together," Sugar said in a matter-of-fact tone.

Toby reared back, looking me sternly in the eyes. "Talk to me, Maddy. You sure as hell didn't hook up with Kaleb, did you?"

I was taken aback by his accusing tone. I sniffled, wiping tears off my face unsure of how to respond. Tara pushed a cup of water toward me. I took it, drinking half. I set the glass on the table and inhaled a shuddering breath.

"I didn't know he was your best friend, Kaleb Knight." I dropped my head, shaking it. "I only knew him as Storm. I mean, I knew his name was Kaleb but didn't think he was the same person. They look nothing alike."

Toby squeezed his eyes shut. He always did this when stressed or thinking. "But how? Where? When?"

"I met *Storm* two months ago at The Bullet. Neither of us knew each other's full names. He knew me as Madeline. I met him as Storm. A month ago, I discovered his first name was Kaleb. I was already in love with him. It all makes sense, now. My heart knew him before my mind did."

"You can't be with him, Maddy. He's the president of an outlaw MC. He's the reason, Tommy…" Toby snapped his mouth shut.

My gutted twisted, hearing Tommy's name. "What? What were you going to say?" Something felt off with Toby's reaction to *everything*.

He shook his head. "You can't be with him."

"Bullshit. I *am* with Storm—his mark is on me." I grabbed the back of my neck.

"What do you mean his mark is on you?" Toby stood from his

chair as if ready to kick Storm's ass.

Sugar shot Toby a dirty look. "A tattoo, hothead."

"I'm his old lady. Him being Kaleb Knight changes nothing!" Excruciating pain stabbed my heart. *I'm his unless Kaleb decides to end it.*

I doubled over in my chair, holding my stomach. *What if he doesn't want me anymore?*

My heart couldn't take it. I couldn't bear losing Kaleb a second time. Not after giving him my body. Not after *we* loved each other so completely.

I would do whatever it took to make sure I kept him.

CHAPTER TWO

STORM

I rode my Harley down one gravel dirt road after another, reliving the night my life changed forever. After what felt like forever, I wound up at a lake I'd never been to before. It was after eleven o'clock. No one was out this late, just me and the night critters.

I fuckin' felt slashed open, bleeding out of my chest. To add insult to injury, a storm crashed down on me. I nearly skidded into a ditch twice. Lightning lit up the sky.

Just like that night.

As the rain poured on me, I was transported back to the day I killed Tommy. I wasn't at Lake Garrison–drunk off my ass with Toby, wanting to get laid on grad night. But it felt the same. Rain and thunder used to trigger me, sending me spiraling back to that day. It took some time but I'd worked through that shit. Compartmentalized it. When the anniversary of Tommy's death rolled around in June, I'd let myself grieve. I'd drink myself stupid and drown in the guilt that I never got over. Knowing who Madeline really was made me weak. It broke me.

All the memories roared back at the club's party. Gut-twisting guilt I'd lived with for over a decade shredded me to pieces, right in front of little Maddy Hamilton. She witnessed my destruction. As I rode my bike, I only sunk deeper into the depths of hell.

I was a fucked up man.

Rain always brought my demons to the surface. It put me in a foul mood. Why did it have to fuckin' rain on the night I discovered Angel was the sister of the boy I killed?

Why did the universe have to suck some major ass?

I faced the lake, squatting before I dropped my ass onto the soggy grass. How did I not know the woman I'd fallen in love with was that little firecracker?

Well, she sure as hell didn't look anything like the skinny little kid who used to follow me around with stars in her eyes. Fuck no. Little Maddy had grown into a beautiful, effervescent woman.

Thinking about it now, little Maddy had been quite the smartass back in the day. A stubborn, determined firecracker exactly like my Angel.

How did I not see the similarities?

I hadn't told her my last name and she hadn't told me hers. Was that normal? Why hadn't it ever occurred to either of us?

If I had known from day one, would we be where we were today? Hell no. I killed her brother. I wouldn't have had sex with Madeline or fallen in love if I knew her true identity. I sure as hell wouldn't have put my mark on her or made her my old lady.

Fuck. I had to do something.

If I'd known who she was in the very beginning, Angel wouldn't be mine. I would be the same guilt-ridden, angry, empty man I was before she appeared on stage beneath the bright spotlight.

It fuckin' killed me to imagine never being with her again. How could I, though? Not after what I'd done to her brother, her family…

to her.

A renegade tear slipped out the corner of my eye. I flicked it away as the roar of motorcycles disturbed the quiet I desperately needed. I'd only been here a short time. Maybe thirty minutes. I knew my brothers would come for me after the way I took off.

Sugar had followed me to my bike, begging me to talk to her, begging to know what was going on. But I couldn't deal and told her to leave me the hell alone. Not my finest moment.

Since I had my phone, my brothers could easily find me with the tracking app all club members were required to keep turned on. I couldn't disappear like I wanted to. Shoulda left my phone to get some fuckin' peace.

Not long after the engines shut off, I heard boots sloshing through the wet ground. I was sure Track was one of them. He was my closest brother and would always find me. Go to the ends of the earth, if needed.

Two sets of boots appeared, one pair on each side of me. Track and Lynx sat on the wet grass and exhaled relieved breaths.

My brothers gave me time and space to process. It was what I needed most. I appreciated their understanding.

"Tell me what you need, brother." Track pushed a flask into my hand.

I removed the cap and took a long pull, welcoming the burn. "Don't need nothin'."

"Bullshit," he hissed.

I took another swig of whiskey. Track knew the guilt and shame flowing through my veins. My other brothers didn't know all the details about the first person I killed. Uncle Matt had said they didn't need to. Maybe if they had, they wouldn't have revered me as much. They'd know what a savage piece of shit I really was for ending the life of a young boy.

We sat in silence for a while as I drank. There wasn't anything to say. My past finally caught up with me, just when I found a woman who meant everything to me. Who loved me unconditionally. I had peace and happiness for the first time in twelve years. Now I had more torment than ever before.

"You need to talk to her." Lynx's irritated voice cut through the quiet like a chainsaw.

"No." I ground my back molars.

Track tapped his thumb on his knee. "She's worried about you."

"She doesn't need to be."

Lynx elbowed me. "Don't shut her out, man. She's a good woman. The best woman any one of us assholes has ever found." He snorted and elbowed me again. "You don't give someone like her up. She loves you, brother."

I tried to ignore Lynx, but the fucker always talked sense. It made it hard to tune him out.

Did Madeline love me? It felt like she did, but we never said the L-word. Until tonight, I never thought we needed to. I claimed her and put my mark on her. She was my Angel. The only woman I wanted to share my life with. Who I wanted to have my babies. Her sweet voice swirled in my ears while I thought about her confession of stopping her birth control. She could be pregnant right now.

Track tapped out a message on his cell phone. "Raul wants to know what you want him to do with her. Her brother and girlfriends are still with her. Sugar too."

"What do you mean, do with her?" I kept my gaze on the lake so my brothers didn't see my glossy eyes. Even with them sitting beside me, I felt empty and alone.

Track put the phone down. "You want him to let her stay at the club? In your room?"

"She's my ol' lady. She bears my mark, for Christ's sake. The clubhouse is her home." I squeezed my head between my hands.

"But if you want her gone, he'll get rid of her. Make her leave,"

Track went on. I nearly punched him in the mouth.

"She didn't deceive you, man," Lynx cut in.

"I know…" I gritted out.

"Then what's keeping you from going back to talk to her?" Lynx fisted his hands, getting defensive for Madeline. He had a soft spot for her. Hell, everyone did.

I turned toward Track. "I can't see her right now." I swallowed down bile before it got into my throat. The very thought of being face to face with Madeline made me nauseous. "I need time. Move her into a guest room and tell her not to bother me. I'll call her when I'm ready."

Track nodded and stood with his cell phone in hand. "I'll handle it."

"Stubborn motherfucker," Lynx muttered. He didn't know the half of it.

For a dozen years, I'd kept my emotions buried. Locked away under the weight of extreme guilt and regret so I wouldn't experience any joy or happiness. I punished myself for Tommy's death, believing I didn't deserve anything good because of my greatest sin.

I hated myself for being the selfish little prick who was more concerned about getting laid than the fear in a boy's eyes. I should've cared more about his well being. Cared more about his family. The little girl who adored me. My selfish actions destroyed a family and broke the hearts of four people I cared about.

Since then, I had kept relationships with anyone other than my brothers one-dimensional… Madeline changed everything.

I never considered love, marriage, or children… *until Madeline.*

I never needed a woman… *until Madeline.*

How could I live without her when I fuckin' needed her more than the air I breathed?

I took another drink and fell onto my back like a drowned rat. I stared at the inky sky. A life without my Angel would be bleak and dismal.

Stupid-ass tears battled to be set free. I blinked them back, trying to hide how pathetic I was.

Madeline's parents would never want her with me. When I killed Tommy, everything had changed, and I was shipped off to my Uncle Matt here in Minnesota. Seeing Mr. and Mrs. Hamilton would open old wounds. I didn't want to hurt them any more than I already had.

I killed their little boy, for Christ's sake.

Darkness swallowed me whole. I didn't deserve the love of a good woman, especially not Maddy Hamilton's. Even if she found it in her heart to forgive me and still wanted me, how could I let her? Being with me was dangerous. Now that I knew who she was, I worried I wouldn't be able to love her right. What if something were to happen and I couldn't think clearly enough to protect her? What if the monster I locked deep inside came roaring out of me? I didn't know what I would do. Finding out who she was changed everything. I couldn't put her in jeopardy. Mr. and Mrs. Hamilton already lost one child because of me. No chance in hell would I let them lose another.

I loved Madeline more than life itself. She deserved so much better than me. It would kill me, but I had to let her go.

After two hours of drinking and sitting in silence, we returned to the clubhouse. All the partygoers had cleared out. No one saw my wet, weary ass trudging upstairs to my room. Even Sugar wasn't around. I was confident she'd be back in the morning.

I stripped out of my clothes, leaving them in a wet pile on the bathroom floor. I hung my cut to dry on the hook behind the door. Turning on the water, I stepped into the shower. I washed off quickly, fighting away the memories of when Madeline and I showered together.

Feeling heavy, I toweled off and crawled into bed. My heart hurt something fierce as I crashed on the pillow. I turned on my side and punched the mattress over and over as I smelled her.

Everywhere.

In the air. On my pillow. On the blankets. It was as if Madeline was here with me. My gut twisted as a razor-sharp pain permeated my chest. I felt wholly destroyed. Pathetic. Like a loser.

I sucked in a breath, tossing back the sheet, and sat on the edge of the bed, gripping my head between my hands. I jerked when my cell vibrated on the nightstand.

It was her. She'd already texted a few times, but I hadn't let myself read them.

But now I was a messed-up motherfucker. A glutton for punishment as I grabbed my phone and opened the messages.

Angel: Please come back. Nothing will change between us. NOTHING

Angel: I'm losing my mind. Please come back.

Angel: Raul said you need space. My heart is shattered. Is it because I'm Toby's sister? Why should it matter? What we have is real. Don't throw it away.

Is it because I'm Toby's sister?

Madeline didn't know. She didn't have a clue I was the one who killed Tommy. If she did, she wouldn't want me. Why hadn't her family told her?

Nausea hit me with a vengeance. I bolted for the toilet and threw up my guts. When Madeline found out I was the reason Tommy died, she would hate me forever.

I retched again into the porcelain, choking out tears.

My Angel would hate me and she wasn't ready to find out why.

CHAPTER THREE

MADELINE

I stared out the window into a black, nothingless. I couldn't feel anything. Not even my heart beating in my chest. Every part of me was numb as I sat in what used to be my living room before I moved out of the trailer park to live on the KLMC compound. My emotions were all over the place. I was heartbroken, then angry. Confused, then worried.

As if I wasn't already devastated, I wasn't allowed in our bedroom. Raul had said Storm needed time and tried to show me to a guest room in the basement. He might as well have ripped out my heart clean from my chest. I'd told Raul to go to hell. If I couldn't sleep in *my* bedroom, I wasn't staying at the clubhouse. I didn't care if I pissed off Raul or anyone else. They had no power over me.

After some heated words with my brother, Raul and Hero didn't stop us from leaving. Although Raul did order a prospect to go with us.

If I thought my heart couldn't break anymore, I was severely wrong. Not long after we got to Tara's place, Toby sat me down to tell me what *really* happened twelve years ago.

Discovering Storm was Kaleb Knight, my childhood crush, was only half the madness. The man I loved was *responsible* for my brother's death. I could hardly draw in a breath as I cried. I was in agony. But not for my brother, Tommy. For Storm… Kaleb. KC.

Toby squeezed my hand. "It was an accident, Maddy. A horrible, horrible accident."

I nodded, wiping my eyes. "Maybe so…" I inhaled a shuttered breath. "But I know Kaleb. Death by his hand would never be considered a tragic accident. All this time, he's carried unbearable guilt. It made him angry and closed off. I saw it in his eyes every day we were together but he hadn't told me why. God, Toby. Twelve years he's lived with this pain."

Then I came into his life. I was his light, his Angel. He must have come undone knowing I was the sister of the boy he killed.

"I know he didn't mean to hurt Tommy," Toby continued. "We were all screwing around at the lake. Drinking and having a good time. Kaleb and I dared Tommy to jump in naked. It was a dumb dare, but Tommy was so chicken shit about the fish trying to suck his dick. We'd had such a long, stupid laugh about it." Toby dropped his head and shook it. "We were tired of waiting on Tommy. We had plans with girls on grad night."

A small smile tugged at the corner of my mouth as I wiped tears off my face. "Typical."

"I'd told Kaleb one way to get on with it was to toss Tommy's ass into the lake, and so he did. Tommy struggled against him, but Kaleb was stronger. When he launched him into the water, I thought I heard a thump but wasn't sure where it came from. It was storming, bad." Toby stopped and inhaled a deep breath. He closed his eyes, shaking his head. "Dammit, if I could rewind time. I do anything to bring him back."

I squeezed his hand as he'd done to mine a minute ago. "You

don't have to do this." I really didn't want to know how my brother died. It hurt too much to open this up after a dozen years had passed.

"Yes, I do. All these years later, when I hear the crack of a bat hitting the ball, I flashback to the night Tommy died." He hung his head in his hands. "It was my fault too. We were being assholes and it cost his life."

"Oh, God." I covered my mouth, utterly horrified.

"I can't watch baseball because of it." He sniffled, rubbing the back of his hand across his nose. Toby always loved baseball. "When Tommy didn't pop up out of the water as he should have, Kaleb and I freaked out. Kaleb jumped into the lake to search for Tommy, but it was too damn dark and pouring down rain." Tears streamed down Toby's face, just as mine returned. "I swear it was an accident. I swear. We never meant to hurt him."

I bobbed my head, swallowing and sniffling. "I know, I know." I reeled Toby into a firm embrace.

We held each other for the longest time crying. Once we calmed, I had some questions of my own. "Why didn't anyone tell me how Tommy really died?"

"Mom and Dad thought it was best you not know. You were so young, Maddy. You didn't need to know Tommy's death was because of Kaleb and me. He drowned, that was the truth, but nobody wanted you to be reminded of it each time you saw us."

I dried my tears with a tissue. "But I would have understood it was an accident."

"Didn't matter. Mom and Dad gave the order, and Kaleb and I followed it." He blew his nose, then gulped a glass of water.

"Why did he leave right after the funeral?" I remembered it like it was yesterday. Kaleb had kept me tucked into his side through the church service and burial. He'd held me while I cried, not once shedding a single tear of his own. Even so, pain and grief dwelled in his stormy gray eyes.

Kaleb had taken care of my every need. Tissues, punch, food, comfort. He never left my side. When it was over, he'd hugged me and apologized, kissing the top of my head. I'd felt better having him with me and had looked forward to the next time I saw him.

Except I never saw Kaleb Knight again.

"Do you remember Kaleb's dad, David, was the president of the motorcycle club in Garrison?"

I nodded.

"The locals were spreading lies in town about Kaleb murdering Tommy as an initiation into the club. They didn't know shit about how the club brought in new members, but it sure as hell wasn't by murdering innocent people… innocent kids."

"Oh my God…" My stomach churned.

"To defuse the gossip, Kaleb's dad sent him to his uncle. I never knew where." Toby balled up his tissues, jaw tight. "I've only heard from Kaleb twice since he moved away. When he was in the marines, he sent me a long letter apologizing for destroying our family. He took all the blame. Knowing Kaleb, he'd kept it on a low simmer inside him, so he'd never move past it."

"I'm certain he's been punishing himself every single day since Tommy died." It broke my heart to think of Kaleb living in his own personal hell. "When was the second time you heard from him?"

"Back in June. He called asking for help with his security system. He said he'd found himself a good woman and wanted to make sure she was safe. He sounded happy, liked he'd finally dealt with his demons." Toby considered me for several beats. "I'm guessing you had everything to do with it."

"Maybe." I shrugged, drying my eyes with a tissue. But I knew it was the truth. "Is it weird?"

"Maybe." A small curl to his lip appeared. "But you're a grown woman now, a beautiful woman. I can't say I'm surprised Kaleb fell for you. Although I'm shocked as hell that you fell for a biker. When did a beard and ink appeal to you?"

My cheeks warmed. It was strange talking about my romantic life with Toby. In all my life I never had. It was more strange that he used to be best friends with the man I loved. "It only appeals to me with him. So... you came to help him?"

"Yes. I wasn't going to pass up the chance. I'd missed the hell out of him. Gotta say I was shocked to see he lived in the next town over from you."

"It's crazy that I never saw him before two months ago." I gazed out the front window, wishing Kaleb would magically appear at the door.

"Storm..." Toby snickered. "His road name fits him."

"It does. I only call him Storm when others are around. He's Kaleb to me when it's just the two of us." I rubbed my hand over my heart. The ache was increasing the longer I was apart from my man.

He playfully elbowed me. "So, you two are serious?"

"Yes. I'm in love with him. But I'm not sure how he feels about me after all this." A lump formed in my throat, again. "I don't want to lose him."

Toby studied my face for a beat. "Why do you think you'll lose him?"

"He's walked away from me before because he said I deserved better. Now he knows I'm Tommy's little sister. It's gotta be killing him." My chest rattled with emotion but I held back the tears. I was tired of crying. "I can't lose him over this, Toby. I can't."

"What do you think you'll do?"

"Well, he said he needed space and didn't want me in our room, so I'm going to stay here until he talks to me. God, I hope he wants to work through this." I twisted my hands together, tossing up a silent prayer. I didn't want to live without him.

"Isn't he going to be upset you left the compound?"

I worried my bottom lip, feeling a twinge of nervous flutters in my stomach. Kaleb would be furious I left, but I refused to say in a guest room in the basement.

"That's his tough shit. He should've sucked it up and talked to me. He shouldn't have kicked me out of our bedroom." My face heated. How could Kaleb push me away so quickly?

"Damn, Maddy. When did you become a badass?" he teased, probably trying to lighten the mood. It didn't work, though. I felt utterly lost without Kaleb.

"I'm not really a badass. I'm trying… I'm just so…" I felt like I couldn't breathe. Like my world was falling into a black abyss. Fear paralyzed me.

Toby patted my knee. "It'll be okay, Maddy."

"What if it's not? What if Kaleb shuts me out forever? It's just the kind of thing he'd do, y'know."

"I know, sis. Believe me, I know…" He sagged into the sofa and held my hand. He was always so strong, even after losing Tommy and Kaleb on the same day. It broke my heart knowing he had to keep the truth from me all this time. Maybe I could've helped him like he was helping me now.

CHAPTER FOUR

STORM

"**W**hat the fuck you mean she left?" I bent at the waist, hand on my hip, my heart about ready to burst from my chest. I never wanted Madeline to leave the compound. She was mine. Bore my mark. The Dirty Hunters were still around, hiding like filthy roaches. We hadn't found their nest. She was in danger.

"You didn't say she couldn't leave, and we're not technically on lockdown," Raul explained in the kitchen. Tina sat beside him at the island, along with Track. Thank God no one else was around to witness my rage. Especially Sugar, after the way I treated her last night. The fear and confusion in her eyes had killed me. I hurt too much over Madeline to give two fucks about my aunt.

"And you didn't think to tell me she left?" I clenched my fists. Idiots. They should have told me.

"No. I didn't." Raul held a stoic expression.

"You said you needed time. That's what she's giving you." Typical Track, trying to be the voice of reason. "Let her be with her friends and brother while you pull yourself together."

I stalked back and forth. "She's supposed to be here!"

"You kicked her out of your bedroom," Track bit back.

"It was her bedroom, too." Tina tilted her head, narrowing her eyes. "She's really hurting, Storm. You just ran off and then Track sent a message she wasn't welcome in her home."

I glared at her. "Have you spoken to her?" I tightened my fists, hating myself for making my Angel feel unwelcome in her home.

Tina sighed, drumming her nails on the island. "Not since last night."

"And?" I clamped down on my back molars, ready to blow any second.

"And what? How about you get over yourself and talk to her?" Tina scooted off the barstool. "I'm not your personal messenger. Call *your* woman if you want to know how she's doing." Tina sighed, shaking her head as she left the kitchen.

You could've heard a pin drop after Tina handed me my ass. I deserved her vexation. I didn't like it, but she was right. I should call my woman. I was just too damn afraid to find out she hated me.

"There you have it. Go talk to her." Raul carried his coffee mug to the sink. "Need me for anything else? Looks like I've gotten you plenty angry this morning."

"No," I grunted.

"You know how to find me." My VP left the kitchen, probably to chase after his wife and kiss her. I knew what that felt like now. That feeling of not being whole when I wasn't with my girl.

Fuck, I missed my woman.

I growled, putting my elbows on the counter and my face in my hands. I wasn't worth shit without Madeline. How did I get to this point? A poor fucker who couldn't eat, think or breathe without his woman in the building, safe in his care?

A throat cleared. "Wanna go for a ride?"

I grunted at Track.

"I'll wait for you outside." He gripped my bicep, his black eyes bore into mine. "At least text her. You didn't see her last night after you left. Her tears broke my damn heart."

I raised my head to look at him.

"You're a lucky son of a bitch, Storm. If I had a woman who cared half as much about me as Madeline does for you, I'd feel like the luckiest asshole in the world. Your woman was out of her mind with worry. She begged me to find you." He put his hand on my back. "She'd go to the ends of the earth for you." He exhaled, digging his hands into his jean pockets. "I envy what you have with her."

"I'm scared, man," I told him honestly. "She doesn't know I'm the one who killed Tommy. When she finds out, she's going to hate me." I gripped my stomach as it churned.

"It was an accident. How many times do we have to go through this?" A growl rumbled in Track's chest.

I pinched the bridge of my nose. I knew Track was tired of my same old song and dance. Couldn't help it. I was fucked up over Tommy's death.

Track exhaled a frustrated breath. "What happened to Tommy was an accident. Maybe Toby told her the truth. Has she tried to call or text?"

"Yeah." I dropped my head into my hands again.

"Today?"

I raised, putting my hands on my hips. "A text this morning asking me to call her."

His intense expression relaxed as if he was relieved she'd called. "There you have it. Call her."

"What if she doesn't know? I can't go through all that with her."

"Maybe she does know, and she still wants you."

"I'll text her." I removed my phone from my back pocket.

Track laughed, leaving the kitchen. "Pussy…"

Whatever. I still needed time to process all this shit. I just preferred to do it with Madeline in the building.

Storm: You weren't supposed to leave. You need to come back.
Angel: Are you going to talk to me?
Storm: I've got a lot of shit in my head. I need time.
Angel: I'm not coming back until you agree to talk to me.

Goddamn stubborn woman!

Storm: My mark is on you. You're my property. I want you here!
Angel: Don't go all caveman on me. I assume you mean in the guest room?
Storm: Yes. I need time.
Angel: No

Fuck! If she was here, I'd paddle her ass for defying me.

Storm: Come back, and we'll talk this evening.
Angel: I'll think about it.

I just might explode. This woman would be the death of me. All I could do was agree and pray she came to the clubhouse later.

Storm: I'll be out until 5

I trudged out to my bike. Track was on his, talking to Hero. Madeline didn't reply to my text. I'd be lying if I said it didn't piss me off even more. If she didn't come home today, I didn't know what I'd do. Probably go haul her ass home *like a caveman*. I rolled my eyes.

For the next couple of hours, Track and I kept to the outskirts of town. Out on my bike, with the wind blowing in my face, taking in the scenery soothed me. The only thing I could think about was

Madeline's tears. I hadn't seen her cry much in the last couple of months. It killed me that she was crying over me.

Toby texted, wanting to meet for lunch. I didn't feel like I had a choice. He'd come all the way here to talk to me. Wasn't right to blow him off even if it was tearing my soul apart, finding out about Madeline. We needed to talk about the various security projects the club needed. Toby had a tight schedule.

CHAPTER FIVE

STORM

Track and I headed to Casitas, the Mexican restaurant in Bastion, to meet Toby. The club managed its security. Maria, the wife of the owner, kept a booth reserved for the club's exec members.

My leg bounced under the table as I waited for my old best friend to enter the restaurant. I wished I hadn't cut him out of my life. Toby and I had been thick as thieves when we were young. We'd spent all our free time together, galavanting around town like we owned everything within the city limits. Those were some of the best years of my life—the good old days.

It had been the Hamilton family who mended the brokenness inside me. I felt worthless and unlovable after my mom abandoned me. What kind of mother leaves her child behind? I couldn't get past the feeling I was why she left. My fuckin' father never told me different.

I'd turned into a spoiled brat, being the only kid in the club. Everyone treated me like a little prince. My "uncles," the members of the club, let me raise hell. They taught me how to fight, shoot a gun, and ride a motorcycle. They had said they were preparing me to become part of the Legion.

When I was old enough, they taught me all about sex. Fuck knows I'd seen and experienced a lot at the clubhouse with the club whores.

"Stop shaking your leg. People are starting to notice," Track whispered.

I put my hand on my knee to stop it. "My nerves are going nuts." I took a long pull of my beer, but it wouldn't do shit to calm my racing heart.

"I'm sure you have nothing to worry about."

The bell on the entrance door rang as Toby entered. The asshole was dressed in gray slacks and a white button-down shirt. His sleeves were rolled up to his elbows. Toby strutted in confidently, turning heads as if he were a goddamn celebrity.

I stood when our eyes connected. Toby's blue depths raked over me with a cocky curl to his lip.

"Well, you grew into a scary and ugly motherfucker." Toby reeled me in for a brotherly hug and slapped my back. "You look good, Kaleb. I'm damn happy to see you."

Jesus, his genuine tone hit me like a ton of bricks, slamming onto my chest. This was how all the Hamiltons had treated me. Like I deserved love. I hadn't realized until now how much I missed them. It made sense now how Madeline could calm the smoldering storm inside me... she was a Hamilton.

We pulled apart and slid into the booth.

"Beer?" I offered.

Toby clasped his hands on the table. "That'd be great."

I raised my bottle, catching Maria's attention. "Three."

She nodded with a smile.

I hiked an eyebrow. "You look good, Mr. Businessman. Clean-shaven even."

Toby laughed. "My job comes with a dress code. Much like your own, aye?"

I chuckled, tugging on the collar of my cut. "Standard uniform." I jerked my chin toward Track. "This here is my road captain, Track."

Toby shook Track's hand. "Good to meet you." He turned to me. "So the president of the club. Crazy shit. I remember you saying one day you'd be president."

"Yeah. It didn't go down quite as I planned. Several years back, my Uncle Matt lost his battle with cancer. I was voted in to take his place."

A pained expression appeared on Toby's face. "Damn, I'm sorry. I know how much he meant to you."

I nodded, a tightness forming in my throat. Maria brought the beers and we ordered our food. Toby talked a little about his job and how it took him around the world. I was proud of him. He'd always been the smarter one out of the two of us.

"Enough about me. Go ahead. Ask." Toby took a pull of his beer. His demeanor changed as he narrowed his eyes. It was as if a dozen years hadn't passed. Toby still knew when I had something to say.

I asked the one question burning on my tongue. "How is she?"

He set his bottle on the table and cocked his head. "Do you actually care?"

"Fuck," I muttered. "Yes, I care."

"Then why'd you push her away?" Toby's gaze hardened. I felt Track's on me too.

The restaurant was busy with the lunch crowd. I let my eyes wander around the dining room as I drank my beer. Maria and another woman rushed around, delivering baskets of chips and salsa to tables. All the while, I could only think of one response.

I leveled my gaze on Toby's. "She deserves better."

He ripped off part of the label on his bottle, nodding. "Maybe, but she wants you."

"And that doesn't concern you? I'm the president of an outlaw MC. I have enemies. We've been dealing with a lot of shit from a nomad club. They're trying to take over our territory. Shit, they've even been to her house. Why do you think I called you?" I slammed my hand down. "She's better off without me."

"Sounds like she needs you to keep her safe." Toby gritted his teeth and fisted his hand on the table. He wasn't wrong. Madeline did need me to keep her safe.

I dragged my hand across my cheek. "If you felt that way, why'd you let her leave the compound?"

"Man, don't throw this shit on me. I only discovered you were with my little sister last night." Toby guzzled his beer.

"She doesn't know I killed Tommy. Once she knows the truth, she'll hate me." I rubbed my sweaty palms on my thighs. Talking about Madeline put me on edge, not knowing what she thought of me.

"She knows."

I blinked several times. "What?"

"I told her about it last night. Stop saying you killed Tommy. You're such an idiot." Toby sagged in his seat. "It was an accident. We were both there. You never would've hurt him on purpose. I know it. You know it. Stop with the 'I killed him' shit."

"Thank you!" Track threw his hands up. "I never believed he killed your brother, but I only knew his side." He turned toward me. "You gotta let it go, brother."

"I can't." I pinched the bridge of my nose, focusing on Toby. "I destroyed your family. You were all so good to me. You took me in when I didn't have a mother around and treated me like a Hamilton. I broke your happy little family. I hate myself for it."

"Why'd you finally call me after all these years?" Toby's question threw me for a loop.

I could tell Toby didn't like dwelling on the past, but it was alive in me. "What do you mean?'

"You called wanting to get together. After not hearing from you in a dozen years, you sounded happy. It was because of Maddy, wasn't it?" He searched my face, making me shift in my seat. His eyes were hard. "Having her in your life lifted the crushing weight of guilt you placed on yourself, didn't it? Having her in your life set you free, didn't it?"

"None of it matters. She's Tommy's little sister." I didn't deserve to be happy or in love when Tommy's life was cut short by my hands.

"She's my little sister, asshole." He leaned forward in his seat. "You're breaking her heart. I'm not okay with that. If she loves you, don't screw it up."

"You're seriously okay with us being together?" I cut my eyes to his. Leave it to Toby to not complicate things. It was how all the Hamiltons were. They were kind, understanding people. Accepting, non-judging, and loving. Dammit. Those were all the qualities Madeline stole my heart with, along with her sexy curves, sultry voice, and those baby blues that sucked me in. No wonder I fell in love with her.

"If it's what you both want, you have my blessing. Not sure my parents would feel the same, but everyone knows Maddy does as she pleases." The corner of his lip curled.

I chuckled. "Don't I know it. Your sister has given me hell from the very beginning."

Damn, I loved her.

"I bet she has. She's smart, independent, and strong. She's going to fight for you." Toby put his elbows on the table and leaned toward me, leveling his gaze on mine. "You want her fighting for you, brother, because the moment she stops, you've lost her for good. You think long and hard about if you want her before making any rash decisions."

The ache in my chest eased up and I could breathe a little better. No question I wanted, Madeline... *Maddy*. There was nothing to think about. I loved her and didn't want to go through life without her.

I only hoped she wanted *me* because I sure as hell wanted *her*.

CHAPTER SIX

MADELINE

After Toby left, I moped around the house until after lunch. He told me he was meeting Kaleb for lunch. As much as I wanted to go with my brother, I knew better. He was in town to help the club with their security and train Grizzly. Toby's time was limited. I wouldn't let my personal issues interfere with the club. Believe me, it wasn't easy staying put knowing he'd see Storm.

Tara rushed around the house packing her suitcase. "I'm worried about you, Mads." She and Steph were going to Richmond to visit a mutual college friend for the week. They'd invited me to tag along, but I declined. I wasn't in the right headspace, and I couldn't leave if Storm wanted to talk. Fixing things with him was my first priority, and I wouldn't miss the chance if the opportunity presented itself.

I waved her off. "I'll be fine. After the shit storm last night, please, go have some fun." My life may have imploded, but I wasn't that selfish. I wouldn't guilt my friends into staying with me even though I was hurting so much I could hardly breathe.

"He'll call. I'm sure of it." She dropped her tote bag at the door. "That man loves you more than his Harley." Tara winked, trying to lighten the mood. "He just freaked out, but you haven't lost him."

"I hope you're right." Not knowing what would happen made me physically ill. I felt like a drug addict going through withdrawals. My skin was clammy, my heart raced unbelievably fast and I couldn't stop shaking. I didn't sleep last night and couldn't eat today. I didn't want to live without him. "What if I don't have a choice? And he ends it?" I'd be completely devastated and shatter into a million irreparable shards, if I lost Storm again.

Tara dropped onto the sofa beside me, kicking her heels up on the coffee table. "That won't happen, Maddy. But if it did, you'd survive. You're strong, babe. After everything you've been through with Dane, there is nothing you can't handle."

"Death is a kinder alternative than life without Storm." I loved him with every cell in my body. Every breath I took. Every beat of my heart had his name engraved on it.

"Shit, Mads. Now I'm afraid of leaving you if you're gonna talk about death like this." She took my cold hand into her warm one.

I rolled my eyes. "Sorry, that's not what I meant." I sounded like a stupid, weak woman. Extreme and over the top. I didn't care, but I didn't want Tara to worry about me. I wouldn't actually do anything crazy.

Tara squeezed my hand. "Please come with us."

"I can't. Storm said we'd talk when he got back to the club later." No way would I leave town after what happened last night. Tara was right, Kaleb was freaking out. I wouldn't abandon him when he needed me most.

"Oh, please. Make him wait like he made you."

"No, I don't play games. You know this."

Tara checked the time on her phone. "I need to go. You'll be okay? You're sure?"

"I'll be fine." I jerked my chin out the window. "AJ is standing watch."

She nodded, biting her thumbnail. "K. Call me if you need anything."

"Have fun." I hugged her and she rushed to her car.

The quiet swallowed me whole as I wilted on the sofa. My chaotic mind conjured every possible scenario of what may happen when I saw Storm. I hated how my imagination was stronger than my good sense.

Pull yourself together, Maddy. You've got this. Storm is yours.

I rubbed my tattoo, swirling my finger over it. I remembered the day I became Storm's property, felt the heat of his large hands on my body when he held me through the pain. He'd soothed me with sweet words of encouragement. Kissing me often. Art had called us disgusting because we didn't hide our affection. Yeah, we were disgusting alright, disgustingly in love with each other. Always hot and desperate. I wrapped my arms around my shivering body. I ached for his touch, for his lips on mine. Needed to hear him call me Angel.

I didn't do well with conflict. For most of my life, I played nice to avoid drama and confrontation. When I grew into a teenager and started dating, I was the sweet, *agreeable,* girl next door.

Not anymore, though. I wasn't the girl I was back in my hometown of Garrison, South Dakota. Or even the woman I was when Dane and I were together. Being sweet and non-confrontational had cost me big. Dane not only manipulated me, but he verbally and physically abused me, knocking me around when it suited him. He forced sex on me, cheated because I was "awful" in bed.

He nearly destroyed me.

Eight months ago, I got out from under him, swearing off men… until Storm appeared out of nowhere like a freaking thunderstorm.

Fisting my hands, I hopped off the couch and paced. I reflected on my life. How did I get to this very place, separated from the only man

I ever loved?

Storm was my person. *Mine.*

I was damn tired of waiting for him to finally be ready to talk. *Get ready, Storm, I can't wait any longer.* I was prepared to launch myself right into the middle of some ugly conflict. Prepared to confront his ass and chew him up one side and down the other for kicking me out of our bedroom. For running away from me.

I was done being agreeable, and all out of patience.

My man was freaking out. Even Track had said as much. Storm needed me, but he was a stubborn son of a bitch.

My mind was made up. I dashed into the bedroom to grab some clothes and hopped into the shower. Fifteen minutes later, I threw on a pair of denim shorts and a blue tee—along with my brown boots, of course.

Grabbing my purse on the way out, I marched to my car, hellbent on talking to Storm. I would make him speak to me. He didn't get a choice in the matter. We were going to settle this shit once and for all, then have mind-numbing makeup sex.

AJ perked up on the seat of his bike and turned down Eminem on his radio. It was always Eminem. "What's up?"

I stared at him for a second. His brown hair was always messy, or windblown from riding his motorcycle. There was a little patch of hair on his chin. He was still so young and fresh. Being a Knight would probably change him. "Going to the clubhouse."

His eyebrows shot up.

"Don't look at me like I'm a crazy woman. Storm wanted me back at the compound so I'm going."

"Okay. I'll follow you."

"Good."

By the time I pulled up to the gate in my little Honda CR-V, my hands were sweating. I held my breath, white-knuckling the steering wheel. It was after 3:30 p.m. If Storm wasn't going to be back until

5:00, what would I do while waiting for him?

Didn't think this through very well, Mads.

Did everybody know what happened? Had word spread throughout the clubhouse that the prez threw his old lady out? Maybe I shouldn't have come. Sugar and Tina were probably around. Shit. I wasn't ready to talk to them.

My heart galloped hard and fast. I hated the unknown.

Dodge waved me through, after talking to AJ. I wasn't sure if I should stop like I usually did, to greet him. Of course, I should. Dodge was a good guy.

I slowed and rolled my window down.

"Hey, Madeline." He stared at me with something strange in his eyes, like he knew what happened. "Storm's not back yet."

"That's okay. I thought I'd hang out with Emilee before he returns. She's leaving for college soon. I'm going to miss her."

He furrowed his brow, then his eyes softened. "Yeah. Leaving soon…" His voice trailed off, appearing to get lost in his thoughts.

This was strange. Did Dodge like Emilee? I never saw them together. Dodge kept to himself. He was Track's younger cousin— tall and tan, like him. The same dark focused eyes, but Dodge never smiled.

I considered him a long second. "I'm thrilled Emilee wants to teach kindergarten. We have a lot in common. Both of us love kids, baking, and *Gilmore Girls*. She's a sweetie. And a pretty girl. Dontcha think?" Dang it, I word-vomited. I eyed his reaction carefully.

Dodge nodded slightly but didn't say anything. He didn't have to because it was in his eyes. There was something more there regarding Emilee.

"I'll let the boss know you're waiting when he gets here."

"Thanks, Dodge. Have a good one…"

The parking lot was mostly empty, save for a few cars and bikes. Typical for a Sunday. I pulled into my assigned spot in front of the clubhouse and turned off the engine. I needed a minute to slow my racing heart.

AJ paused by the entrance. I waved for him to go on without me.

My stomach twisted into knots. Why was I nervous? Storm wasn't even here. It didn't matter to my chest though, it felt like an elephant decided to sit on it. What was happening to me?

It was like the end was nearing as I held my hand to my stomach, trying to breathe through the nausea. My whole body tensed. The end of what? Me and Kaleb? Was he in danger?

I'd grown up in a religious home with two parents believing in God's will and the Holy Spirit speaking to them. Was my uneasiness the Holy Spirit trying to warn me?

What if I didn't get a chance to talk to Kaleb? What if this pain in my chest was a heart attack? These were heart palpitations, right? Oh God, I could hardly breathe. What if I passed out?

I inhaled a deep breath and prayed—anything to steady my heart and calm this fear that something terrible was coming.

I'll write him a note!

If something happened to me, he'd have my last words. *Crap!* I sounded morbid. Whatever, I grabbed the notebook I kept in the pocket of my driver's side door and started writing.

Kaleb, my love,

I have a weird feeling something awful is going to happen. You weren't here when I arrived to ease my fears. On the off-chance I never see you again, I wrote you this letter. God, I hope I'm just overreacting, but I feel it in my bones. Something horrible is coming.

Whatever you're thinking about Tommy's death, stop. JUST. STOP. It was an accident, baby. I know it was. I don't blame you. Toby told me everything. I want you to know, none of it changes the way I feel about you. I still want to be with you.

46

I want to be with you more than anything. Every day I dream about us having a baby and our future together. A life with you is all I want.

I love you, Kaleb Knight. I have since I was a little girl. I will love you until I draw my last breath. Whatever happens today, tomorrow, or years from now, never stop living. Even if I'm gone, keep moving forward.

Yours always and forever,
Angel

A tear streaked down my cheek. That sure sounded like a goodbye letter. I folded the paper in half, stuck it in my notebook, and hopped out of the car. If something happened to me, I was sure Storm would find it.

A guard wasn't posted at the door, so I walked right into the building, making my way down the hallway to the bar's entrance. Storm's handsome face stopped me as I stared at his picture on the wall. There were fifty pictures of past and current KLMC members—several were fallen brothers.

The club's brotherhood was the most beautiful display of trust, loyalty, and love I had ever seen. Many of these men didn't have a family outside of the club. Copper came to mind. I knew he wasn't the only one who'd grown up in the foster care system. Many had heartbreaking stories. Their hard edges and frozen hearts were how they protected themselves. Down deep, they were soft and sweet. Devoted, with the right amount of possessiveness, like my Storm. I admired and respected every one of them.

Hearing a couple of voices in the bar, I peeked my head around the corner to confirm it wasn't Storm's. When I was sure, I went toward the kitchen. He may have said he wouldn't be around until five o'clock, but what if he only told me that to keep me away? What if

Dodge lied and Storm was actually here? I needed to be sure.

I listened at the kitchen door, hearing Tina's quiet voice. A grunt followed. I tried to be stealthy, peering around the corner. Once again, no Storm, just Raul.

That left Storm's—no, *our* bedroom—upstairs. Or he could be in the large garage in the back of the compound. It was where the guys tinkered on their bikes and let their frustration out on a punching bag. For some reason, I didn't think Storm was out there.

I headed for the stairs, thankful it was a quiet Sunday. The guys always partied hard and were hungover the day after a party. At the top of the stairs, I exhaled a sigh of relief.

What's this... I narrowed my eyes, padding down the hallway. Our bedroom door was cracked open. Was Storm here, after all? Hope bloomed in my chest. I was desperate to see my man.

I pushed the door open. The rumpled linens on the bed caught my eye, but still no Storm.

"Baby, it's me," I called, facing the bathroom. The door was partly open. I didn't want to intrude if he was on the toilet.

Tremors rolled through my body, my stomach flip-flopping and churning. Never had I been so nervous. What on earth was going on with me? We didn't have an argument. I mean, finding out who we really were was quite a shock, but it didn't change the way I felt about Storm. In fact, it explained our deep connection.

The door swung wide open.

The earth violently shook.

"He's not here." Carla appeared in a black lace bra and a tiny pair of panties. A smug grin spread across her bright pink lips.

"What are you doing in my bedroom? Nobody is allowed in here." My pulse whooshed in my ears as bile shot into my throat. Wasn't it obvious what she was doing?

"It's Storm's room, not yours. And what Storm wants, he gets. You know that." She slithered toward me like a viper readying her strike. "What do you think I'm doing here, *Angel?*"

"You bitch, answer my question!" Why did I need to hear it from her lips?

"Are you that stupid? You can't see I was taking care of *my* man?" She jerked her head toward the messy bed. "He always comes back to *me*." She laughed, stepping toward me.

Shocked and mortified at what this all meant, I was speechless. Dying inside.

"He had a little business to take care of, ya know. Or maybe you don't, since he made you leave." She snorted, closing the gap between us. "Last night, we fucked until the sun came up. He couldn't get enough of me and my pussy…" Her fake purple eyes assessed me. "He ordered me to wait for him so we could go at it again… He's masterful with his tongue." The bitch shrugged. "But I'm sure you know that."

I swallowed the acid and found my voice. "You two-bit whore!" I slapped the shit out of her face, ignoring the sting. It felt as if the floor dropped out from below me as my world fell apart.

Carla yelped in surprise. "Stop, you crazy bitch!"

"He's not your man, you, fucking whore!" I slapped her again and again, grabbing a handful of her hair in my other hand. I unloaded on Storm's go-to kitten, unable to stop the rage consuming me. I'd never felt such contempt and hatred toward anyone.

I didn't want to believe it—Carla and my Kaleb. My heart splintered and cracked as I yanked on her fake blonde hair—grunting as I jerked her head around.

"Let go of my hair!" Carla screamed. "Let go!"

"I'll kill you! I. Will. Kill. You!" I heaved the words out, tugging with everything I had on the slut's hair. She screamed louder as I bent her in half. All I could think about was Storm screwing this skanky bitch. Driving his cock into this whore and licking her pussy.

I gagged as vomit burned my throat with a vengeance. I held it back because right now, I wanted to kill Carla. Pull every strand of hair out of her scalp. Beat the ever-living shit out of her for touching *my* man.

"What the hell is going on in here?"

Suddenly, I was lifted off my feet. I hardly noticed as I pulled the first blonde clump out. Then a second. And a third. Carla's hair was ripped from my hand. I kicked and thrashed to get free, swinging my hands at the idiot who interrupted my beatdown of that fucking kitten.

I struggled to get at Carla when she was moved out of my reach. Fought with all my might. What was holding me back?

"Stop, Madeline," Track yelled. "Do you hear me? Stop!"

My surroundings returned to focus. I twisted, finding Lynx behind me with his strong arms wrapped around my waist. My chest slammed against my ribs. Bloody scratches were on the top of his hands and my nails dug into them. I'd been clawing at him to get away.

"Oh, Jesus… Fuck no..." Lynx cursed like a madman. Words spewed from his lips, saying everything I couldn't voice. Not when I was dying inside. Dying the most painful death a person could experience.

"Calm down, Angel." He shushed me, dragging me away from Track and Carla.

"Let go of me!" My fight returned. I ripped myself out of his arms. "Don't. Touch. Me."

He put his hands up. "It's okay, babe. It's okay."

"Fuck all of you!"

I ran like my life depended on it, to the stairs, ignoring Lynx shouting to stop and his heavy footsteps. My pulse hammered in my ears, drowning everything out. I made it to the entrance, bursting through the glass doors. I needed to get away from the MC. Get away from anything to do with Storm.

I. Was. Done.

I'd almost made it to my car. Almost. But stupid Lynx was fast.

"No, babe. You aren't leaving like this." His muscular arms went around me, squeezing me tightly.

"Let go… God, please… Let me go…" I begged, pushing on his arms. All I wanted to do was die.

"I can't. Storm would chop off my balls if I let you go, after that shitshow upstairs. I don't know what happened, but you need to stay."

"Isn't it obvious what happened? He had sex with her! The first bump in the road we hit, and he fucks another woman! A kitten! That bitch!" I struggled to get free of his arms, but it was no use. Lynx's grip was unbreakable, and I was far too devastated to keep fighting.

I had never felt so broken. Completely destroyed by Storm's betrayal. Even after he knew what Dane had done to me, he slept with Carla.

He always comes back to me. Carla's words burned through me.

Did he think we were over? Was I the only one truly invested. Maybe Storm was just like his father and would never settle down with *one* woman. Maybe I didn't really know him at all.

I'm such a fool. They can all go to hell.

"Let's get you inside, Angel." Lynx lifted me off my feet and carried me.

I couldn't reply through my wracking sobs. What was there to say, anyway?

Track was in the entry when we entered the clubhouse. I hid my face in Lynx's chest as I cried.

"You need to get here *now*. It's Madeline…" Track was on the phone.

Lynx took two steps up the stairs.

I fisted his cut as fury ignited in me again. Was he insane? Blind? Heartless? "No! Not *his* room."

"Babe, it's your room too."

"No it isn't! Please," I cried out, unable to hold myself together. "Take me to a guest room." As if I'd ever want to be in Storm's room after he had that wench in it.

"But he'd—"

"Please," I begged like a whimpering child. Didn't he care that Storm cheated on me? Perhaps *I* was the fool in this equation. It wouldn't be the first time, but it sure as hell would be the last.

"Take her to a goddamn guest room if that's what she wants!" Track snapped at Lynx. I would be eternally grateful to him.

"AJ! Go with Lynx. Guard Madeline's room."

Guard my room? I was a prisoner now? *Peachy.*

"What happened?" AJ asked.

Lynx grunted, jerking his head toward the kitchen. I was shocked no one else was around—a small blessing. Instead of abject humiliation in front of dozens, it was only in front of a few.

"I don't want to see him," I muttered as Lynx stomped down the steps. His grip tightened around me. Probably in frustration, but I didn't care. I didn't care about anything.

"He's the prez. Can't stop him from going into your room."

Shit. Storm was the last person I wanted to ever see again.

"Room four," Lynx rasped to AJ. "Tell me what you need, Angel." He stopped at the door so AJ could open it, then set me on the bed. Lynx looked wholly undone. His hazel depths appeared tormented, brows furrowed beneath sweat. I eyed the scratches and dried blood on his hands and arms caused by me.

"Don't call me that. My name is Madeline." I gritted my teeth, reaching for the box of tissues. "You're holding me against my will. Let me out of this goddamn place. That's the only thing I need, Lynx."

"Jesus Christ." He scratched the back of his blond hair, eyes darting to AJ. "Grab a few bottles of water." Lynx turned toward me after AJ dashed off.

"No white bread for the prisoner?"

"You're not a prisoner. If you want something else, we'll get it for you." He stared into my eyes with compassion. It didn't matter if he felt bad, he was one of them, a Knight. Loyal to only Storm, the club and his brothers. I didn't truly matter.

"I'd rather die than take anything from any of you heartless, soulless bikers. I thought you cared about me. I thought you guys had at least one decent bone in your body." I shook my head, sniffing back my runny nose. "This is on me for trusting Storm. Just leave me the hell alone."

Lynx blanched as if sucker punched. After marking him up with my nails, I should've felt awful, but I didn't. He was locking me in a room against my will. I hated him and the rest of the bikers for staying loyal to that bastard Storm.

"If you need anything, AJ will be at the door." Lynx dropped his head and left the room. After AJ placed the bottles on the nightstand, Lynx locked the door from the outside.

I launched off the bed. Screaming, I banged on the door, knowing full well it wouldn't do a damn bit of good. I just needed to hit something. Whirling around, I took in the Cracker Jacks Box room. I imagined it was slightly bigger than a prison cell—sans a urinal hanging on the wall.

Fury and heartache flooded my veins. I went to the small window, bending the aluminum blinds to see if I could get out through it. No luck. I screamed again, reaching for the small lamp on the nightstand. I launched it at the mirror above the chest of drawers.

My knees buckled, falling onto the dingy industrial tiles. Carla's sneering face pummeled my mind, driving me insane. Images of Storm touching her, licking her, and fucking her lashed at my raw heart.

Storm. He wasn't my KC... *Kaleb*. The boy I loved most of my life. No, he'd changed.

Today was proof. Kaleb Knight no longer existed. He'd changed over the last twelve years. Not only in appearance, but he wasn't the same person who would protect me with his life. He couldn't be trusted or faithful. On so many levels, he'd shown me what a remarkable man he was when he wouldn't let anyone else see. But my one rule, the one thing I swore to myself I would never stand for ever again, Storm shit on it.

Whatever were his excuses, they didn't matter to me. If he had a weak moment because of learning who I was, if that was what sent him over the edge, I didn't care. If he felt deceived because he thought I knew who he was all along, so he drowned himself in booze and Carla's pussy, I didn't care. He could have all the excuses in the world, grovel, plead and cry, but I would never, ever forgive him. Never take him back after this betrayal.

I was done with this whole outlaw MC life. Done with their *I am the king* misogynistic life. If Dane taught me anything after treating me like shit and beating the crap out of me, it was nobody would rescue me from my situation. It took me months to realize I had control of my life. After I'd mustered every ounce of courage I could, I got out from under his abusive fist. I was done being a weak doormat and his punching bag.

Just as I was done with Storm.

Crawling on the floor to the bed, I hoisted my weary body onto it and curled into a ball. Tears soaked the pillow as I mourned the loss of my childhood crush, KC, all over again.

Storm could burn in hell with *his* kitten.

CHAPTER SEVEN

STORM

I ran into the clubhouse with Hero on my heels. My heart hammered against my ribs, fearing the worst. Had Madeline been hurt? Did the fuckin' Hunters get the drop on AJ? Christ, were they both dead? Goose flesh spread over my arms at the thought. If my Angel left this earth, I was sure I would've felt her soul die. Ours were intertwined. We were soulmates. I would've felt her life floating away to the heavens. Wouldn't I?

"What happened?" I scanned the entrance but nothing appeared amiss. I wasn't sure whether to be relieved or terrified.

Track and Lynx looked sidelong at each other. My chest tightened, pulse whooshing in my ears.

Track sneered. "You fucked Carla! How could you? I thought you cared about Madeline. Hell, I thought you loved her." The disgust on his face had me rolling my hands into fists. I swear he wanted to rip my head clean off my neck.

Fuck Carla? I couldn't have heard him correctly. "The fuck you say, brother?" I went face to face with him, clenching my jaw, nostrils flared. "How dare you accuse me of such bullshit!"

Sugar and Tina appeared, stopping when they saw Track and me.

Track eased back half a step. "You weren't with Carla last night?"

"Oh Jesus, what's going on?" Sugar got between us, putting a hand on my chest. I ignored her, keeping my deadly gaze on my so-called best friend... my brother.

"No, I wasn't with that bitch! Where the fuck is this coming from?" Had I just entered the fuckin' Twilight Zone?

When Track called saying I needed to come back to the clubhouse, he never told me why. Nor did I ask. All I heard was *It's Madeline*. I sprinted out of the gunshop with Hero, and left Toby with Grizzly and Wolf, to bust my ass back to the clubhouse.

"Somebody talk to me." Sugar tapped my chest to get my attention. Her calm voice did nothing to dampen the rage bellowing in my chest.

"Not now, Sugar." I moved her out of the way.

Track glanced at Lynx as he ran his hand through his hair. On a nervous exhale, he said, "Carla was in your bedroom in her bra and panties."

"What?" I roared, seeing red. How in the hell did she get into my room? I always locked the door. Had I been so fucked up, I forgot? No, locking the door to my room was second nature.

Lynx moved forward. "And... Madeline found her inside. Carla taunted her about y'all fucking and how you wanted her to wait for you in your room."

Sugar and Tina both gasped, covering their mouths.

The whooshing in my ears went deadly silent. My stomach twisted so tight I couldn't breathe. Every part of me went numb. This was so fuckin' bad.

"What. Else?" I gritted my teeth.

"Madeline lost it on her, Prez." Lynx shook his head. "She

slapped the shit out of Carla, scratching up her face and pulling her hair out. She threatened to kill her. I'd never seen any woman so angry before." He grabbed his arm.

I caught a glimpse of dried blood. "Where is she?"

Lynx growled. "Carla's in the quiet room. We didn't know what to do with her." The quiet room was a padded cell used for brothers who were out of control.

"I don't give a shit about Carla. Madeline! Where's Madeline? In my room?" I took three long strides toward the stairs. No one answered. I turned around with an expectant expression. "Well?"

Track sighed, bracing his hands on his hips. "In a room downstairs. She doesn't want to see you."

"Well, she doesn't have a goddamn choice!"

"Storm." Sugar grabbed my hand.

Track stepped in front of me, blocking the way to the dorms. "Take a minute to calm down. She's in a bad way. What she saw, what Lynx and I saw looked real. It destroyed her, man."

"She told us to all fuck off and ran out of the building." Lynx squared his shoulders. "I stopped her just before she got into her car. She struggled and fought me with all she had." Lynx gripped the back of his neck, eyes suddenly glossy. More marks were on his forearms. "Then she broke, Prez."

I breath hung my lungs, going face to face with Lynx, our noses almost touching. "Why didn't you tell her it was a mistake. A lie? Why didn't you tell her I didn't fuck that bitch?"

"Because it looked like you had," Lynx hissed through clenched teeth.

"Motherfucker!" My voice boomed as I shoved him in the chest and raised my arm to punch him in the fuckin' face. "You let my woman believe I cheated on her!" I swung, but Track caught my fist.

"Calm down, Storm." Track gripped my bicep, holding me back. Hero stepped in front of Lynx. "If you'd seen what we saw, you would've believed it."

"The hell I would, brother!" I ripped my arm away, grunting like an angry bull. "I'd trust my brother before some club whore! I'd always have his back." My face was on fire. I felt like I would explode.

"Storm, you need to calm down. Please, honey." Sugar moved in front of me.

Track exhaled a heavy breath. "Shit, man. I'm sorry. It looked real."

"Well, it wasn't. Now move the fuck out of my way so I can see my woman." I glared at him, clamping down on my back molars. I'd never felt an ounce of rage toward Track before, but if he didn't get out of my way, I'd break his goddamned face.

He stepped to the side, and so did Sugar. Knew my brother was smart.

"Go soft on her, man," he muttered as I passed.

What did he think I was going to do? Unload on her? *Asshole.*

If anyone knew what seeing Carla in my room would do to Madeline, it was me. Christ, I couldn't believe this happened. What fuckin' timing after I kicked her out of our room like a heartless, selfish prick.

Goddammit! I could choke Carla for what she did. I should've made her leave last month like I wanted to, but instead, I'd listened to my woman.

I slowed my heavy steps as I entered the hallway leading to the dorm rooms. The dim lighting overhead unnerved me. *Dead man walking* whispered in my ear as the hairs on my nape prickled.

A prospect guarding Madeline's room made me sick. She didn't belong locked up.

AJ shot daggers my way. He must've believed I cheated too. How could everyone think so little of me? Or maybe they all thought so highly of my woman. They were clearly *Team Madeline*. I should be pissed as hell, but I wasn't. I wanted them to protect her, even from me.

"AJ."

"Prez." He squared his shoulders, leveling his gaze—the hate in his eyes burned me up. He'd proven himself worthy of becoming a Knight. I'd make sure he got patched before the year was up.

I placed my hands on my hips. "How's she been?"

"Sobbing. Throwing shit. Whimpering. Begging me to let her out." His eye and jaw twitched in time. I didn't miss it when he rolled his hands into fists. He'd rue the day he took a swing at me.

"I didn't cheat on her." Why I felt compelled to convince AJ, I wasn't sure. I was the president. I didn't owe anyone an explanation, but I hated the disgust on my men's faces.

AJ didn't respond.

I stepped closer and repeated myself in a firmer voice. "I would *never* cheat on Madeline."

The tension radiating off AJ disappeared. Still, he didn't respond, only giving me a short nod. He unlocked the door and moved to the side.

"You can go," I told him as I entered, noting the door latching closed behind me. Madeline was curled into a tight ball on the twin bed, her back to me. She didn't move.

My heart seized, the air in my lungs evaporating. A paralyzing pain hit me dead in the chest at the sight of my broken Angel. The regret I felt was more severe than after Tommy died. Both offenses were because of *me*. The blame was on *me*.

I should've made Carla leave months before Madeline ever entered my life. I shouldn't have run off last night. I sure as hell shouldn't have kicked Madeline out of our bedroom. I was the worst fuckin' man alive.

Trepidation flooded my veins as I inched toward her. This was dire, no question, but she had it wrong. I needed to fix this. I couldn't lose Madeline. Not over a lie, not even because she was Tommy's sister.

I'd been a fuckin' idiot for pushing her away again.

Madeline's eyes were closed, her beautiful face red and blotchy. A wet circle was on the pillow, soaked with her tears. God, she was breathtaking. My Angel...

I took in the room, assessing the damage. A mirror above the dresser was shattered. A lamp from the nightstand seemed to be what broke it. The lampshade was deformed, the lightbulb was also destroyed. She really had gone off the deep end.

"Angel," I whispered, lightly touching her hair with my fingertips.

She jolted, eyes flashing open, and flew off the bed to the opposite side of me. She shook her head rapidly as her swollen, red eyes went wide.

"Get out!" she screamed. "Get. Out!"

"Baby, you have it wrong." I raised my hands in surrender, to assure her she was safe.

"No! I was there." Her body shook. Rage flashed in her baby blues. "I saw Carla and the bed..." She gripped her stomach, bending at the waist. "You... you ma... make... me s... sick..."

It killed me to see her shaking and stuttering. *Christ, I'm a bastard for letting this happen.*

"I want... t... to go... home." She wiped her face, keeping her eyes downcast, wincing in pain. Her voice was hoarse. She looked *and* sounded broken.

"You are home, Angel."

"Don't! Call me that!" she yelled at the top of her lungs, grabbing a water bottle off the nightstand. She lobbed it at my face. I ducked just in the nick of time and it hit the door.

I exhaled a frustrated breath. "Angel..."

"You sonofabitch! Don't... don't... call me that..." Tears streamed down her face. She pointed a trembling finger. "Are you...

so… so fucking… heart," she paused, putting her hand on her chest, gasping for air, "heartless. Don't you... c, care... an ounce about me? Tormenting me after you betrayed me with… with her!" It tore me up to see her turn into the wall and choke back her emotions. Like the strong woman I knew her to be, she fought her tears with all her might. She hated appearing weak, but a sob ripped from her lungs despite her efforts.

Her agonizing wails gutted me. Never had I heard anything so painful and heart-wrenching. I couldn't let her go on believing I fucked Carla, but she was so damn stubborn and unwilling to hear me out.

Only one thing left to do: *make her listen.*

I caged her in, placing my arms on either side. Pressing my lips to her temple, I pushed her head against the cement wall. My body surrounded her, not giving her an inch to move or fight.

"My stubborn Angel. You will fuckin' hear me out. Right this fuckin' second." My words came out in an angry, unyielding voice. Couldn't help it. I was beyond frustrated, not with her but with the situation. "I am *never* letting you go. Do you hear me? Never." I leaned into her body, inhaling her unique scent. "You're mine, mine since you were a little girl. You'll forever be mine. Just like I'm yours, *Maddy*. I. Am. Yours."

Her body trembled as she cried, but she didn't fight or yell. I believed she wanted me to prove I didn't cheat. I could. *Right the fuck now.*

"Let me prove I didn't touch that bitch. Prove our bed is still sacred. Only you have ever been in it, Angel. I told you the first night you stayed at the clubhouse. I didn't lie to you. You gonna let me show you what you saw was a lie?"

I kissed her head, waiting for her reply. I didn't like her taking so long, but she'd be reasonable. She'd want proof.

Madeline stared me dead in the eyes, a challenging glint in hers.

"Knock yourself out," she whispered in a ragged breath.

I pressed my lips to her forehead, holding them in place. Sassy little shit. I loved this side of her. The fighter, take-no-shit side. She pushed me at every turn. Made me want to be a better man. Worthy of her love and trust.

"Okay, Angel. Let's go to my office." I took her hand, and she let me. She was giving me a chance.

I opened the door, finding AJ still standing there. His eyes ping-ponged between Madeline and me. He seemed to be searching her face. A tight jaw and fisted hands told me he was ready to defend her. It pissed me off when it shouldn't.

"Thought I told you to leave." I went toe to toe with him.

AJ held his head high. "I stayed for Madeline."

I pressed my lips thin. "But I—"

Madeline squeezed my hand, stopping the ass-chewing I was about to give AJ. She was right. Now wasn't the time to get into it with the prospect. She was my priority.

I nodded, leading Madeline away. As we passed through the kitchen, she kept her head down. Sugar and Tina were at the island.

Sugar stepped toward us. "Storm is she—"

"Not now, Sugar."

CHAPTER EIGHT

STORM

We made it into my office without anyone else seeing us. I shut the door and tugged Madeline by the hand over to my desk chair. Dropping into it, I patted my lap: her spot. I hated seeing her so wrecked. Her baby blues were puffy and red, and her face was blotchy. It looked like she'd been pulling on her hair.

Madeline was still the most beautiful woman despite her gaunt appearance. After not having her in bed last night, I needed physical contact. Shit, I'd become a needy son of a bitch, but I didn't give a fuck.

I needed my woman and was confident she needed me just as much.

Madeline tilted her head as if considering my request. I didn't like it. My stomach tightened as I dragged my hand over my beard. If she said no, I wasn't sure what I'd do.

"Come on, baby. I swear to you, I didn't cheat. You don't have to hate me."

"But last night, you didn't want me." Tears pooled in her eyes.

"Angel, it wasn't about wanting you. I always want you. Let's deal with one issue at a time, okay? First, I need to prove nothing happened."

I turned on my laptop and reached my hand out to her. She perched herself on my lap like she had dozens of times before, taking my hand in a strong hold. Her back was to my chest, my chin rested on her shoulder. I closed my eyes for a second, just breathing her in.

She elbowed me like she was worried I was falling asleep. "Storm."

Ouch, that hurt. "It's Kaleb, when we're alone."

"Just get on with it."

Christ, I didn't like her calling me Storm. But I'd let it slide this time, we had enough to worry about. I typed in passwords to retrieve video footage from the security cameras in our bedroom.

"What's this? Your room?" Her head turned toward me, putting our lips a breath away. I stole a quick kiss. She narrowed her eyes, then rolled them like the sassy little shit I loved. There wasn't an ounce of surprise in her expression. She knew I'd always take every opportunity to put my lips on hers.

"Yes. It's *our* room. Before Uncle Matt died, he gave me some advice. Valuable advice I'm now very glad I took. As president, we should be able to trust our brothers. But sometimes, a bad seed comes into the club. To protect me, as he suggested, I installed video cameras that only I know about. Should something happen to me, I have a letter for Track with the passwords to all my accounts and the surveillance cameras."

"Oh, no." She worried her lip between her teeth. "Are there videos of us having sex?"

I chuckled, stroking her thigh. "Shit yeah, baby."

She gaped, her mouth in a sexy 'O.'

"Don't worry, no one will ever see them except us."

"Promise?"

"I promise." I stole another kiss, but this time I lingered a second or two longer. Melting into her soft lips, tasting her sweetness. She didn't push me away. I could finally breathe again. "Now, let's start at midnight. We'll scan through the footage until we get to Carla."

"I hate her," she muttered in a low voice.

Me too, Angel.

"She's gone, baby." Well, she would be once I restored Madeline's trust. Then I'd go to the quiet room with Lynx, and we'd take care of Carla once and for all. Not by killing her. Only if she pushed or threatened Madeline would I do away with her. It was tempting, but I didn't kill when I didn't have to. Even if the world would be a better place without her.

On the feed, we observed me returning to the clubhouse. I stiffened, recalling what a shitty night it had been.

"Wait." Madeline put her hand on mine to stop me from fast-forwarding. "Let it play."

I shifted in the chair, stomach roiling. Goddammit, I didn't want her to see this, but what else could I do? I was trying to prove my innocence, but…

"Kaleb." She swallowed, placing her hand on her chest. "Baby, were you…" Her voice trailed off. "I made you cry?" Her arm hooked around my neck, and she buried her face in it. I wrapped my arms around her small body and held her.

"A grown-ass man like me can shed a few tears." I'd missed her so damn much. I was fucked up, hating myself all over again for hurting her. "Don't tell my brothers, okay?"

She pulled back, taking my face between her hands, and brushed her thumbs over my beard. My heart raced with anticipation. I didn't want to push myself on her, but I was desperate for a real kiss. She claimed my lips. I let her have her way for once. Her small tongue curled with mine, drawing out moans from both of us.

Madeline broke away much too soon. She needed to see what happened with Carla in the room. I felt her hesitation. It would resolve the minute she knew I was still hers.

"Your secret is safe with me, I promise. Crying doesn't make you weak." She pressed her forehead to mine. "My heart hurts, seeing you so miserable. The bed is a crumpled mess because you thrashed all night."

"I couldn't get comfortable. I missed the fuck out of you. If you don't want to see me miserable, then don't ever leave me."

"Kaleb..." she breathed out my name. "I believe you, but I just... I need—"

"I know. You just need to see for yourself. I get it. I want to see what the bitch was doing in our room."

We got to the footage of Carla. It was after two in the afternoon. I hadn't been in our bedroom since before 8:00 a.m.

Fuckin' Carla had picked the lock like a pro. I knew I hadn't left it unlocked. I never forgot to secure it.

Carla snooped through our drawers, ripped holes in some of Madeline's panties, stuffing them back into the drawer and sniffed my shirts. What a nutjob.

"Jesus..." Rage exploded in my chest when the crazy bitch took her shorts and tank top off and rolled around in our bed in her bra and panties. She got herself off, humping my pillow and crying out my goddamned road name.

"Turn it off." Madeline shuddered in my arms. "I'm going to be sick." She held her stomach, drawing in large amounts of air and blowing it out.

I reached for the trash can beside my desk, in case she threw up. "I'm sorry, Madeline."

"No, you didn't do anything. It's obvious the video isn't fake. She's wearing the same bra and panties I saw her in. I believe you." She clasped her hands in her lap. "I'm the one who's sorry. I should've trusted you. It's just when I found her…" She dropped her head, shaking it.

"Look at me." I lifted her chin, putting us eye to eye. "I get it. I see how it looked real to you. For that, I'm sorry."

She giggled a little. "Look at us both apologizing when neither of us did anything wrong. It's all Carla's fault."

"Yeah, well, I want to get to the part where you beat the shit out of her." I couldn't imagine my sweet girl in a catfight. I needed to see it for myself.

"Oh, God." She buried her face in her hands. "I lost it, Kaleb. I really lost it."

I scrolled through the footage. Carla even cracked the door open after she was finished masturbating on the bed. Like she was hoping Madeline would find her. Sure as shit, Madeline called my name when she thought I was in the bathroom. Carla walked out with a smirk on her face.

As I watched it all unfold, Madeline hid her face in the crook of my neck. I understood why she couldn't watch it. To her, it was a low moment of losing her cool. She wasn't proud of it, but I was fuckin'proud. *My* woman kicked Carla's ass.

I exited out of the app, logging off of my computer. I rubbed my hand up and down Madeline's back. "Finished."

"I need you, Kaleb Knight. I want you to make love to me, but our bed—" She trailed off.

"It disgusts me too. Tomorrow we'll buy a new mattress."

"Really?" Her face brightened.

"Hell yeah. Tonight, we can stay in the room you were in." Going to a nice hotel wasn't an option with the Hunters still around.

"How are we going to sleep on a twin bed? You wouldn't even fit on it alone."

I chuckled, squeezing her ass. "I didn't say sleep. I said stay in. Tonight, we're having all night make up sex." I wiggled my brows.

Madeline threw her head back, laughing. Her voice was hoarse and sexy at the same time. "Shouldn't we talk about what happened last night? You found out I'm little, gangly Maddy Hamilton. You know, the one who used to annoy you."

"You never annoyed me. And Angel, there ain't nothing gangly about you." I kissed her nose. "What about you? What I did to Tommy." The muscles in my neck coiled as I feared her reaction. All this time we'd been together, loving each other, and I'd been the one who shattered her perfect little family. I'd broken my Angel's heart. "Sure, you want to be with me?"

"Jesus, Kaleb. You didn't kill my brother. Toby assured me it was an accident. Yes, what both of you did was wrong. But you didn't mean to hurt him."

"I swear to you, I never wanted him to get hurt. I'm so sorry, my little firecracker." I ran my thumb along the curve of her jaw.

"You remembered." She cradled my face in her hands, stroking the apples of my cheeks.

"Of course I do."

"Can I call you KC?"

"No. KC doesn't exist anymore. It's Storm in public. Kaleb when we're alone." I kissed her nose. Talk about a blast from the past. My mom had called me KC because I'd been conceived in Kansas City. Mom was weird like that. I'd stopped going by the nickname after moving to Minnesota. I'd wanted nothing to do with my home in Garrison.

She pouted. "Fine."

"I love you, Maddy. Goddamn do I love you." It felt freeing to finally give her the words. I wasn't sure why it had taken me so long.

Happy tears filled her eyes. "I love you too, Kaleb. I have for most of my life."

"Now, I don't need to be jealous of the dude who owned your heart." A good thing, too. I almost had Grizzly hunt him down for me.

"Nope, you sure don't because it's you. It's always been you."
She pressed her lips to mine.

"Toby gave me his blessing."

She reared back, eyes wide. "He did?"

"He just wants us to be happy."

"Well, then, make me happy and take me to bed." Her arms went
around my neck. "Make love to me, Kaleb."

"Shit yeah, Angel. I'll make love to you all night long. I love
you. Damn, I love you so much." Giving her the words felt fuckin'
fantastic. I couldn't seem to stop saying them.

"I love you, Kaleb Knight. With all of my heart. God, I want
you." She kissed me again. Nothing compared to hearing them said to
me.

"We'll fuck right here in my office." I nipped at her bottom lip,
slipping my hand under her shirt and cupped her breast. I brushed
my thumb over her taut nipple, rocking my hips forward. Eager to be
inside my woman.

She hiked an eyebrow. "Have any kittens ever been on this desk?"

I grabbed the back of her head, pushing our foreheads together.
"Never. I never brought any of them into my personal space. Now take
those tiny shorts off so I can fuck you."

She shivered. "I love it when you're bossy."

"I love it when you obey me." I dropped my hands, gathering
the hem of her shirt. Pulling it over her head, I dotted kisses across
her shoulder, dragging my lips up the bend of her neck. I was hard as
stone, aching to be deep inside her.

Madeline's fingers went to the back of my neck. Her nails
scratched along my skin in her unique, arousing way, sending electric
bolts straight to my cock. "I'm still shocked you're my Kaleb." Her
lips ghosted across mine. "The teenage boy I drooled over. Talked to
when no one could hear me. When I got older, I touched myself under
the covers, staring at your senior picture under the warm glow of a

flashlight. I missed you so much after you left town. I didn't think I'd ever see you again."

"Fuck, Angel." I captured her lips as a swell of indescribable emotions flooded my heart.

She sucked on my bottom lip, then captured it between her teeth. A bolt of lightning shot down my spine as she released it. "I still have the picture tucked in my wallet."

"Seriously?" I was stunned she'd kept it so close to her.

"Mhm." Her baby blues darkened. Arousal rolled off her in massive waves, turning her chest red.

The air in my office crackled and sparked, heating up like an inferno of lust as we stared into each other's eyes. We grabbed for each other at the same time, frantically kissing and removing each other's clothes. I couldn't believe Angel was little Maddy *firecracker* Hamilton. The things I'd done to my woman. I should burn in hell for them. But Madeline didn't want me to burn. She was the bucket of water to the flames of hell I thought would scorch me forever.

Madeline straddled me on her knees, easing onto my cock. "Kaleb!" She threw her head back, forcing us to break our kiss, and moaned in ecstasy. I didn't want to let go of her delicious lips. They were my drug of choice. All I'd ever need.

"Goddamn, Angel. Your pussy is warm and tight." I raised her up by the hips and pushed her down on my cock.

We began an unhinged pace, rushing for the finish line. It was like we wanted to launch into orbit together and never stop floating from the high.

Madeline panted, riding me fast and hard. I bucked my hips, watching her titties bounce. Her dark hair flew around me, skin glistening with beads of sweat. Madeline always looked hotter than hot when we fucked like wild animals.

"I'm close, baby," I grunted.

"Me too."

"I want you to come with me."

"Okay."

We picked up our speed, the walls of her pussy clamping down on my dick.

"Now!" I drove into her forcefully, grabbing her face and smashing my lips to hers. I blew my load as her warmth covered me. I smothered my girl with kisses, emptying what felt like gallons of sperm into her. Twisting my fingers into her long, silky hair, I tugged her head back and sucked on the hollow of her neck. I felt the sensations running through her as she pulsed around my cock.

I would never tire of this... of us. Never desire anyone else, only this woman. My woman. My Angel.

"I love you, baby. I promise to show you every day just how much."

Her lip trembled, eyes pooling with tears as she smiled. She hooked her arm around my neck, pressing her voluptuous body into my chest. "I love you, Kaleb. Always have, always will... until the end of time."

CHAPTER NINE

MADELINE

Finding out our true identities had shaken the foundation of our relationship. If Kaleb had chosen to let his guilt over Tommy consume him, he would've pushed me away.

The lies and deceit of a bitter, hateful woman shattered me from the inside out like never before. If Storm hadn't had proof he didn't touch Carla, I wouldn't have believed him. Before yesterday, I trusted Storm with my heart. I hated how I let the damage Dane had done control me. It was like Dane still had power over me.

I should've known Storm would never betray what we had. I should've seen right through that lying bitch. Even if it looked real. *So goddamn real.*

Today was a new day and I refused to let Carla steal another second of our joy. We were still us, especially after all we'd been through.

Kaleb and Madeline.

Storm and Angel.

Wrapped in each other's arms after a full night of making love, I was sure we looked ridiculous on the small twin bed. I couldn't imagine any of the hulking men around here sleeping on one. Talk about a comical, *Saturday Night Live* worthy sight.

Due to the emotional and physical exhaustion we'd been through, we slept soundly. If I was honest, I loved the cramped quarters. Storm held me through the night as if I was an extension of him—a vital organ. I felt the same way. He was the oxygen in my lungs.

I had suggested getting bigger beds for dorms while we were going at it. My stubborn man's only reply was *I'll consider it.*

His warm lips brushed across my shoulder. "You awake?" His low, lusty voice caressed my skin as he dotted kisses on my neck.

I trembled against him. "Of course I am. You're poking me in the ass."

He snorted, moving his hand over my hips. His finger slipped down my crack.

My eyes went wide. "Kaleb?" My heartrate leaped into a gallop. What was he doing?

"Hmm?" He never went near my secret hole. I didn't like it.

Why am I getting wet?? Clenching? Why is my clit throbbing?

"I want this puckered hole, Angel. I want all of you."

Tears burned behind my eyes. Good and evil warred within me. Storm was good. He would rather die than hurt me. He loved me more than life itself. He wouldn't hurt me. Wouldn't force me to do something I didn't want to do.

Dane was evil.

I gasped for air as if my face was smothered into the mattress, his hand wrapped around my neck to hold me in place as he forced his way into me. But Dane wasn't here, he wasn't taking what he wanted. Yet the flashback assaulted me as if it was real, reminding me of the trauma I'd been through while in the arms of the man I loved with all my heart. *No. Stop. Please...*

"Angel?" Kaleb's low voice cut through my thoughts.

I swallowed the emotion building in my throat. "Yeah?" Dammit. I didn't sound okay. Stormy gray eyes assessed me faster than I could clear my throat.

"Baby, what's wrong?" He swiped a traitorous tear from under my eye. "We don't have to. I'd never force anything on you."

My chest rattled as I tried to hold back more tears. Storm would kill anyone who forced sex on another. It was why I was afraid to tell him everything Dane had done to me. Hitting me was enough to warrant Storm's wrath. The other stuff… It terrified me what he might do to Dane.

If Storm went to prison for murder, I would be lost without him.

"Angel, talk to me." He tipped my chin, so our eyes met. He searched my face as if trying to read my mind. "Does this have to do with Dane?"

Damn, he had a keen eye.

"I want you to have all of me. I do but—"

His cell phone rang on the nightstand. It couldn't have been later than eight in the morning. I was sure it was important. Storm rarely received early calls.

"I'm sorry. Hold that thought." He frowned, reaching for the phone and answering it. "Sheriff?"

Was it Sheriff Hendricks or Bush?

I couldn't make out what the person on the line said, but it wasn't a pleasant call, judging by the waves of tension rolling off Storm's body. I felt every bit of his reaction, holding him this close.

"I'll be there. Yeah." He ended the call, eyes stricken with grief. "I'm sorry. I need to go."

"Is everything okay?"

He dropped a soft kiss on my lips and stared into my eyes. "No. I want us to finish our conversion. But later, okay?"

"It's okay. Go do what needs to be done." The call saved me

from telling him about Dane. But at what cost? Worry marred Storm's handsome face.

"I wanna know the rest." He hiked a dark brow. "When I get back, we'll go shopping for a new mattress. Then we'll talk. I want you to tell me why your body went rigid."

He was scary observant. I nodded.

He kissed me softly. "Okay, I need a quick shower."

"What about Carla?"

He froze as he stood. "Don't worry about her."

"But where is she? I don't want her here anymore."

"Consider her gone."

"Gone? Gone how?" I gripped my stomach. I might hate Carla, but I didn't want any of the guys to harm her after what I did yesterday.

Storm cradled my face and kissed the tip of my nose. "We won't hurt her. We'll make her leave the state."

Relief washed over me as I watched him pull on jeans and a T-shirt.

He eyed me. "Will you be okay? Do you wanna go upstairs with me?"

"I'm fine." The thought of going into our room while it reeked of Carla made me feel ill.

"All right. I'll be back in an hour or two." He gave me a chaste kiss and dashed out the door. If he felt I needed to know what was going on, he'd tell me.

My stomach churned, remembering our conversation before we were interrupted. Storm wouldn't let me off the hook. He wouldn't forget.

Rolling into a ball on my side, I clutched the pillow to my body. I inhaled my man's scent into my soul. It reminded me of riding on the back of his Harley, leather and his natural musk blowing in my face. Sheer perfection. If I thought a little harder, I could taste his whiskey on my tongue.

If I told him Dane forced anal sex on me after beating me up, he would lose his mind.

Lose. It.

Lying or hiding the truth was wrong. But it literally made me sick to think about what Storm might do. Maybe Sugar and Tina could help me navigate through this.

I exited the community bathroom and bumped into a wall of muscle.

"Ah!" I stumbled over my feet.

"Angel," Copper gasped, catching me before I hit the floor.

"Fuck, didn't see you." Ire dragged his hand over his face. "You okay?"

"Mhm. I'm fine." I steadied myself against the wall. "I should've been watching where I was going."

"Naw," Ire shook his head, brow furrowed as if pissed. "It's my fault. I should've seen you coming." This poor beastly-sized man had been struggling since the attack. He blamed himself for what happened to the women and couldn't get past it.

"Really, I'm okay." My assurance didn't seem to matter.

The three of us stood in the hallway. I rocked on my heels, thumbs in my short's pockets, glancing at Copper. Ire stared ahead with a blank expression for several awkward seconds.

"Heard about your beatdown. Think you can give me some tips on fighting women off?" Good ol' Copper broke the ice.

I giggled, nearly peeing my shorts. "Please. You love all the attention." I'd only seen the kittens purring around him but I was sure he got that everywhere he went.

Copper puffed out his chest, running his thumb along his jaw. "Suppose you're right. Where you headed?"

"Oh. Right. Upstairs. I should… I should be going." I smiled softly and darted toward the stairs. They were right behind when I padded into the kitchen. They each grabbed a cinnamon roll on their way out.

Sugar acknowledged me first, wrapping me in a warm embrace. "My God, girl. I'd tear that bitch to shreds if I could get the key to the quiet room."

I hugged her back. "What's the quiet room?"

Sugar stilled. "Oh, um. Storm's never mentioned it?"

"No." I arched my brow. Goose flesh spread across my arms. Something about the way she said *quiet room* gave me the heebie-jeebies.

"Come sit and have coffee. My nephew said to take care of you." Sugar ushered me over to a table and poured me a cuppa.

Tina made a pouty face, giving me a gentle hug. "How are you really, honey? Storm said you were better, but you know men, they can be utterly oblivious sometimes."

I sat, reaching for the mug. "I'm better. Mostly."

"Mostly?" Sugar eyed me, taking a seat.

"You don't sound very confident, honey." Tina was on my other side.

These women were my new tribe. Sugar and Tina were like mentors teaching me what they'd learned. They had nearly twenty years of MC experience. Tara, Steph, and Kim hadn't seen much of me over the summer. They didn't understand my new MC life. Hell, I hardly understood it.

"Well, Storm and I are good. He proved his innocence." I sipped my coffee.

"I'm so glad," Sugar said. "Tina and I will help you disinfect the room. It'll be cleaner than a hospital." She winked.

"Thanks, I appreciate it." I bit my lip and tapped my nails on the table.

"Is there something else going on?" Sugar asked, a note of concern in her voice.

My eyes darted around the kitchen, making sure no one was in earshot. "There is something else." I sipped my coffee again, leaving Sugar and Tina hanging while I swallowed. "Something happened this morning in bed. When Storm returns, he's going to want to talk about it." I wasn't sure why I felt cryptic. Tina had been physically abused before Raul. From what little she'd revealed at various times, her experience was much worse than mine with Dane. And Sugar was the most understanding person. It was safe to tell them.

Tina patted my shoulder as if sensing my struggle. "Take your time, honey."

A nervous breath caught in my throat before I released it. "I love Storm with my whole heart. He's my everything. There isn't anything I wouldn't do for him."

Sugar reached for my hand. "We know."

"Except maybe giving up my secret hole…" I whispered.

Sugar blinked her hazel-green eyes, squeezing my hand. "He would never—"

"Oh, I know," I blurted to assure them Storm didn't pressure me. "I know he would never hurt me. It's not that I don't want to… I think." A weird tremble rolled down my spine. "It's just, well, Dane." I grimaced as a stabbing pain pierced my heart.

Sugar covered her mouth with her free hand, eyes pooling with tears. "Jesus, Angel. I don't want to assume anything. Did he hurt you there?"

I was so glad I didn't need to spell it out. I nodded and sipped my coffee.

A murderous spark flashed in Sugar's eyes. "I'll chop off his dick." She growled. "How'd he like a banana shoved up his ass?" Her reaction wasn't even close to how Storm would react. She was intense, but my man would detonate like an atomic bomb.

Tina was silent and I had a feeling this hit close to home for her.

I put the mug down. "I'm afraid of what Storm will do if I tell him. I'm not saying I'll hide it from him. It's just fear of what he'll do, y'know?"

"I've never told Raul the extent of abuse I went through. He never pushed me about it." Tina rubbed my arm. "I'm not saying you shouldn't tell Storm."

I smiled softly at Tina. "Thank you. Were you able to get past, you know, and do it with Raul?"

Tina shook her head. "We've never had back door sex. He never tried, and honestly, I'm relieved."

I drank my coffee, mulling over what to do. Storm made it known what he wanted but he also assured me we didn't have to.

"He already hates Dane. What if my abuse gives him a reason to unleash holy hell on him?" I glanced between Sugar and Tina. "I'm afraid he'll kill Dane and go to prison. I shouldn't be, though, right?" I waited for a reply and didn't get one. "Storm will control his anger, right?"

Sugar and Tina stared at each other. I didn't need an answer.

I felt sick.

CHAPTER TEN

STORM

"**S**onofabitch." I seethed, staring at Sheriff Hendricks. We were at our private rendezvous spot, Wennberg Pond.

"We don't know if this incident is related to the Hunters. It could be foul play."

I cut my eyes to him. "She was found in the forest naked and dead, you said. Do you really believe this isn't the Hunters or the shit they're trying to bring into the area?" If he did, he was a goddamn fool. I'd have bet my life the Hunters were responsible.

The sheriff dragged his hand across his face. "I don't know what the hell to think. All I know is, I want Sugar and the boys to stay on the compound until those bastards are gone. She won't like it, but don't give her a choice. Put the club on lockdown or something."

"I'll handle Sugar." I was her president. She respected my authority. Even if she hated staying at the clubhouse because it made her miss Matt, she didn't have a choice.

It was times like this I wished the family wing was finished.

I'd halted construction, not wanting to risk a Hunter getting on the compound with the crew. Sugar would prefer staying in a different building. *"Too many memories,"* she'd said on more than one occasion.

Hendricks stared at the pond. "If I could protect her like you, I'd keep her at my place."

I shook my head. "No, she stays with me. It's what Matt wanted." My uncle made me promise to protect Sugar and the boys with my life. I never broke a promise.

"Appreciate it. Eve and the boys are all I have left." He looked over his shoulder at AJ and Hero. "We need to get these damn Hunters gone."

"Their numbers are dwindling." It wasn't enough, though. This murdered college student was proof.

Hendricks raised a displeased eyebrow. "Yeah? I'd rather they just left the state."

"Me too. But when a fungus doesn't go away on its own, it needs to be eradicated. That shit takes time," I told him. It seemed we fell into our usual ambiguous banter.

He nodded, turning to face his car. "I need to go deal with the homicide. Let me know if there's anything you need."

"Will do. You do the same." I jerked my chin toward Hero, letting him know we were finished.

Jesus Christ. It'd only been a month since the attack at The Bullet. Nancy and Ava didn't file a report, choosing to leave it to the club. I had prospects watching them at their homes. Before they left the compound, Ava told me to not show her rapist mercy. If I got my hands on the enforcer, he'd wish he was never born.

Four hours later, Madeline and I stared at our new bed. We bought new sheets, pillows, and a comforter to go on the new mattress.

I was concerned about her. She'd been off since I picked her up to go shopping. During lunch, she had a hard time keeping eye contact. She had shit on her mind. I suspected it had something to do with this morning.

"Is it me, or does it look bigger?" She placed her hands on her hips.

I sidled up behind her, wrapping my arms around her waist. "It sits a little higher off the ground. But not any bigger than the other king-sized mattress." I kissed her neck.

She dropped her head onto my shoulder, melting into me. "What's the quiet room?"

"Who told you about that?"

She turned in my arms to face me. "Sugar. Is it where you're keeping Carla? Is she still in the clubhouse?"

"No, baby, she isn't. Boxer and Lynx took her home, packed her shit up, and made her leave." I didn't go with them. I wasn't sure what I might do, breathing the same air as Carla. Couldn't risk it after I promised Angel I wouldn't hurt her. I was confident Boxer would handle her. Lynx sure as hell proved he couldn't make her listen on his own.

"How do you know she'll stay away?"

I dropped a soft kiss on the tip of her nose. "Because they scared the life out of her so she'd never return to Minnesota."

"They threatened her?"

"Yes."

"But they didn't touch her?"

I sighed. "No." Why she cared one way or the other about that bitch irritated me. Carla didn't deserve her kindness. My woman had the biggest heart. Incredibly sweet to everyone.

She fidgeted with her nails. "Okay. Go ahead. Ask your question."

I backed her up to the bed so she'd sit. My gut was tight. This woman made me fear the unknown more than I ever had in my whole life. I needed to be gentle with her. Whatever she was going to tell me was probably why she was off this afternoon.

Kneeling between her legs, I took her hand and stared into her eyes. "This morning had to do with Dane, didn't it?"

Just jump right in with both feet, right?

She nodded.

Dammit, my blood pressure skyrocketed. I did my damnedest to keep it in check. I didn't want her withdrawing from me.

"Angel, if you don't want to tell me, I won't push you." The way my gut twisted, it might be better to keep her secrets to herself. *Pussy, I know.*

"No. If we're going to be together—"

I cradled one side of her face. "We *are* together. That's never changing."

"Right." She sighed, but none of the tension in her body disappeared. "I told you Dane was awful to me." She held my gaze. "He made me feel like I couldn't do anything right and sucked in bed."

My jaw tensed. Couldn't stop it or stop squeezing her hand as I gritted my teeth. "Yes."

"He knocked me around a lot. Sprained my arm. Kicked me in the stomach when I'd fall on the ground. Fractured a couple of ribs. He was careful where and how he hit me so my bruises couldn't be seen."

"Fuck." I felt like I couldn't draw oxygen into my lungs. *I will beat the shit out of that fucker for laying a hand on her.*

"When I didn't want to have sex, well… I didn't have a choice." Tears pooled in her eyes as rage engulfed my chest. She took my hands, holding me in place. "Please don't freak out on me. Don't do anything that will land you in jail. I need you."

"Angel, I need you to be clear about this. Are you saying he forced himself on you? Because baby, that's rape." I saw red. Sweat beaded in my hairline, my heart thundering so fuckin' hard it might explode in my chest.

"I don't like to think of it that way." She blinked back her tears.

"What?" I said harsher than I intended. "Don't let this prick off the hook. Did you fight him off? Cry as it was happening? Were there bruises afterward? Did he take... your ass?" I choked the words out as images of that animal hurting my woman pummeled me. Was it possible for my heart to burst out of my fuckin' head? It pounded so hard I was sure it could.

"Baby, please, calm down." Her avoidance confirmed my fears.

I tried to pull my hands away, but she tightened her grip. "Goddammit, Angel. Fuck! Fuck no, he didn't hurt you that way, baby. Jesus fucking Christ... I'll..." I heaved and growled like a vicious animal, unable to tame the raging savage storm inside me.

Madeline threw herself into my arms, hooking hers around my neck. "Hold me. I need you." She buried her face in my neck, pressing her body to mine as if trying to crawl inside me. "Please, Kaleb. I got out. He can't hurt me anymore."

I lifted off the floor, cradling her against me, and sat on the bed. We stayed there, holding onto each other like our lives depended on it. Mine certainly did. My soul cried in agony for what had happened to my beautiful, sweet Angel.

Sexual assault enraged me. Any person who took what they wanted from another was the worst kind of human. When the Hunter raped Ava, it tore me up. Ire still hadn't recovered from not being able to protect her. Not one Knight stood for the mistreatment of women. Sure, we had our kittens, but they wanted to be here. Gave us their bodies of their own free will. Always.

If one said *no*, we stopped. If one of my brothers didn't, he would be dealt with firmly. I ran the club the way Uncle Matt did. We weren't saints by no means. Our moral compass may have seemed skewed by some standards, but we respect others' lives. We only killed when absolutely necessary. We dealt with the worst kind of scum. Had our own rules we lived by. Sexual assault, none of us took lightly.

If Madeline thought I wouldn't take the son of a bitch, Miller, out after hearing what he'd done to her, she was sorely mistaken. I wasn't a motherfuckin' outlaw for nothing. I was a one-percenter. No pathetic, power-tripping deputy with a pencil dick wouldn't get away with assaulting my woman.

"I love you, Angel. Fuckin' love the hell out of you." I kissed her forehead, swallowing down the emotion caught in my throat.

She peered up at me. "I love you too, my beautiful man." She sat up. "But I'm not stupid. You're going to take out Dane, aren't you?"

Damn straight I am. "That's not for you to worry about, baby."

"Jesus, Kaleb. How can you say that? If you kill him, you could get caught. Sentenced to life for killing a deputy. What if I'm pregnant? Or get pregnant. Do you honestly want me alone, raising our child? For *life*, Kaleb."

"You don't need to worry. I won't get caught."

She flew off my lap, her hands gripping her head. "God, you're infuriating! I knew this would happen if I told you the truth. I knew it!"

I got off the bed. "How can you let that piece of shit get away with hurting you?"

"Ever heard of forgiveness? I don't need you avenging a crime I've already put behind me. I don't need you fighting my battles when I already did. I've been free of Dane for a long time now."

"He deserves to pay," I squeezed the shit out of the back of my neck.

"You know what? I'm done talking about this with you." She bolted for the door.

"Where are you going?" I roared, charging after her.

She whirled around, putting her hands up. "Stop!"

I froze.

"I need to calm down. I can't do it here with you."

"Don't walk out that door, Angel. We need to deal with this."

She put her hands on her hips. "You might be the prez of this club. Your club. You call the shots, everyone listens. I obey like the rest in regards to the club. The. Club. When it comes to *my* life, I call the shots! In *our* relationship, we make decisions *together*!" She opened the door.

"Angel—" I hissed, trying to hold back my wrath.

"No! You think about what I said. And don't follow me." She left the room, slamming the door closed.

"Fuck!" I punched it and winced from the pain. Goddamned solid oak door. I paced, flexing my probably fractured knuckles.

I didn't understand her way of thinking—damn, stubborn woman. It was my duty as her man to seek retribution. To avenge my Angel. It was one thing for fuckin' Miller to give me shit and fuck with my life. This was another thing entirely. He didn't get to hurt my woman. Even if I didn't know her back then. She was my little firecracker, the squirt I used to protect from her wild brothers. I would wipe anyone off the face of the earth for hurting her.

I checked my phone to see where she'd gone via the tracking app I put on hers. At least she still had her cell in her back pocket. If she tried to leave the property, I would drag her to our bedroom and turn her fair ass red.

Her locator stopped at the kitchen. Probably to rant to Sugar and Tina about me.

I'd give her some space, then I'd go get her.

And makeup.

Deputy fuckin' Miller's days were numbered.

CHAPTER ELEVEN
MADELINE

Sugar, Tina, and Libby watched me devour a large bowl of chocolate ice cream with sliced bananas, whipped cream, and maraschino cherries on it. It was the closest thing to a banana split I could make in the club's kitchen.

"I'm guessing it didn't go well." Sugar popped a cherry into her mouth. Nobody had questioned me when I blew into the kitchen. Nope, they just watched me build my sweet treat.

I flicked my eyes to Libby, then shot them to Sugar. "No."

I didn't know Libby very well. Talking about my fight with Storm wouldn't be right. Not in front of a kitten, even if I knew Libby was the nicest out of all of them.

Sugar gave me a barely noticeable nod to show she understood.

"So is ice cream your indulgence when emotional eating? I can make sure we have more on hand." Tina laughed, squirting whipped cream on her sundae. "I mean, I'm down with it. But I'll pack on the pounds if we regularly gorge ourselves like this."

"Why was this stuff in the fridge?" I asked, mouth full of yummy deliciousness.

"You're not that naïve, Angel. It's regularly stocked with whipped cream, chocolate syrup, and cherries. Right, Libby?" Tina winked at the kitten.

Libby's face turned the color of a maraschino cherry. "Yeah, the guys claim they don't like sweets, but a fair number of them eat up during sex." The blonde beauty with a button nose seductively licked her spoon.

My eyes bulged, getting her meaning. "Oh."

"Libby?"

A gruff voice came from behind me. I turned to see who barked at the sweet kitten. Grizzly?

"Yeah, Grizz?" She licked her spoon, green eyes shimmering like emeralds.

"I need you. Bring the can of cream." He disappeared down the hallway leading to the dorms.

"Speak of the Devil. I haven't seen him with anyone else lately." Tina arched her brow. Her gaze was locked on where Grizzly had been standing.

"Because he hasn't been." Libby smiled, snatching the can off the table. "I hope whatever upset you, Angel, is quickly resolved. Storm's not the easiest man."

I set my spoon in the bowl and turned my gaze toward Libby. "And you know this how?"

He'd told me he hadn't been with any of the other kittens. He better not have lied to me.

"The only person he's soft with is you. He's madly in love with you, girl." Libby flashed a radiant smile. "Before you arrived, the club was his only focus. And his brothers. He never talked to any of us kittens, like the other guys. If you're wondering, I've never fucked him." She bit her bottom lip. "But a girl would be a fool for not wanting to. Bye." She dashed off.

"Okay…" Tina rolled her eyes. "I'm glad she got called away."

Sugar snorted, swirling her spoon in the bowl. "Don't worry, Angel. Libby's never tried anything with Storm. Not that he'd allow it. My nephew isn't controlled by his dick."

A throat cleared. *Storm.*

"I'd prefer if you didn't talk about my dick." His lips were on my cheek. "Let's talk, Angel," he whispered at the shell of my ear. It always made me melt when he did it.

I tilted my face toward his. "Gimme ten minutes, please."

"You got it." He cradled my face with one hand and kissed me. "Mmm, sweet as ever. I'll be in our room."

"Okay." I smiled, running my tongue over my top lip. I eyed his squeezable ass as he left the kitchen.

"That looks promising." Sugar nudged my arm.

"He's going to kill Dane." My eyes darted between Sugar and Tina. "I told him not to. That I'm fine and have moved past it."

"Oh, honey. Let that thinking go." Tina put down her spoon. "You mean everything to him. We all see it. Retribution is the MC way. Avenging you is what he needs to do, so he'll be at peace."

"But it's not necessary. I don't want him to get caught and go to prison." I wiped my mouth with a napkin. "I can't lose him."

Sugar nodded with understanding in her eyes. "Talk to him. Plead your case. Maybe he'll listen and leave it alone. But if he doesn't, as his ol' lady, you need to support him. Stand by his side."

"Because he's your man and you love him," Tina added.

I steepled my hands under my chin. "I do love him."

"Then you have your answer. We don't live a traditional life, sweet girl." Sugar patted my arm. "Danger lurks everywhere. These guys live to protect what's theirs. And you're Storm's. His property. It's even tattooed on the back of your neck." Sugar collected the empty bowls. "Go to your man and makeup. It'll all be okay."

"I'll go up. Thanks, ladies."

I entered our bedroom and was shocked to see Storm in bed, arms behind his head. No shirt. His magnificent body was on full display. He was a commando man, so no boxers. The sheet dipped so low on his hips, the dark hair of his happy trail was visible.

I clenched my legs together, mesmerized by this incredibly sexy man.

"Angel…" he crooned.

"Hi…" I breathed out, locking the door. "I thought we were going to talk?"

"We'll talk in bed. This mattress needs to be christened." He threw back the sheet, revealing how ready he was for me. The very sight turned me molten with desire.

I padded toward the bed, whipping off my tank top. Kicking off my flip flops, I shimmied out of my shorts and thong all at once. At his side of the bed, his heated depths raked over my body, searing every inch of it.

"I don't want you to go to prison for me." I climbed onto him. Raising up, I braced a hand on his firm chest.

There was no time for foreplay. I wanted Storm inside me, stat.

"I'd die for you, Angel." He palmed his cock for me to lower myself onto it. We groaned together as our bodies became one.

"I'd die with you then."

He took my face in his large hands and guided my lips to his. "I'm sorry."

"I'm sorry, too."

"Tonight, I'm making love to my woman." He kissed me sensually, stealing the air from my lungs, caressing my skin with his rough palms.

It was impossible to stay angry with this man. My heart wouldn't allow it. Not when he loved me so perfectly.

"If I asked you to marry me, would you say yes?" He nibbled my lips, raising and lowering his hips slowly.

My orgasm was building with each deep, penetrating thrust. I could hardly think. "Are you asking?"

He flipped me onto my back, his speed picking up. "No. Just curious what you'd say." He sank deeper, hitting my G-spot.

"I'd say…" My back bowed, on the brink of shattering below him.

"Say what?" He sucked my neck and pinched my nipple between his thumb and middle finger.

"Yes," I cried out as he hit my G-spot again.

"Again." He went balls deep.

"Yes… I'd say yes."

"Fuckin' love you, Angel."

"Not more than I love you." I panted, hovering on edge.

"Come for me, baby." He dropped his mouth to my nipple and sucked for all he was worth.

"Anything you say…"

CHAPTER TWELVE

STORM

Sugar glared at me in my office, her hands on her hips. I followed a lot of Uncle Matt's ways in running the club. He always had church Monday mornings. Said it was to connect with his brothers after the weekend. Made sure everyone was doing all right and on the same page for the week. I did the same. Except we didn't have church yesterday after the clusterfuck with Carla.

By the looks of it, my aunt was not happy. I just might be late for my own goddamn meeting. I expected as much, but Sugar and the boys were staying here whether she liked it or not.

"I promised Matt I'd keep you and the boys safe. You need to stay on the compound."

She paced in my office, twisting her hands. It was a dick move mentioning Matt. Sugar missed the shit out of him—to the point of falling into a funk when anyone brought him up. I didn't have time to draw this out so I used Matt to get Sugar to stay.

She stopped and faced me. "Okay. I don't like it but I understand.

The boys and I will stay for as long as necessary." She twisted her lips. "What're you doing about the dead woman that was found?"

"That's what church is for."

"Right. I shouldn't have asked. I need to pack a couple of bags for the boys and me." She reached for the door handle.

"Take them with you. I'll send AJ and Copper."

She placed a hand on her hip. "Two prospects? Is that necessary?"

"Why are you questioning me?" I had no patience right now. Couldn't help being an ass.

"Fine." She bit her bottom lip. "Before I go, are you and Angel okay?"

Standing from my desk, I stalked toward her. "Yes. You know what Dane did to her, don't you?" I suspected Madeline told her and Tina. I hated being the last to know important stuff about my woman.

Sugar nodded with an almost pained expression. "She told Tina and me a little bit."

"I figured." I jerked my chin toward the door so she'd open it.

"She doesn't want you to do anything to Dane."

"I know." I gritted my teeth. Last night I promised not to go after him. Then I warned Angel if Deputy Miller so much as looked cross-eyed at her, he was done. She agreed. It wasn't like me to be controlled by anyone, but I saw her point. What happened to her was before me.

Madeline was strong as fuck. She'd dealt with her own demons and moved on. I could stand to learn a thing or two from her.

Sugar patted my bicep. "We won't be too long."

I grunted, following her out.

Raul and Track sat at the counsel's table for church. Grizzly was at his desk in the corner. Not only was he my techie guy, but he also helped Boxer setting up security systems.

I raised my chin to them. "I'm really tired of these fuckin' Hunters."

Track and Raul nodded in agreement, their faces solemn. They knew about the young woman who was raped and murdered. I felt awful and responsible for this bullshit.

I dropped into my chair at the head of the long, oak table. There were always carafes of coffee for our morning meeting and sometimes an egg bake Tina made, or breakfast pizzas a kitten picked up at the Stop & Pump on her way to the clubhouse. Other times, Sugar spoiled us with homemade rolls... cinnamon rolls.

Pouring myself a cup of joe, I inhaled the aroma as I took in the room. This was where the council voted a man in or out. Or, in my case, into a new position. We celebrated a newly patched member. Got sloshed after one had fallen. We plotted retribution for an offense against our club and family. It all happened within these four walls.

Since I'd been a member, the club only had one other MC war. Most of the club's dealings were with gangs or the Mafia. I was ready to turn my territory upside-down to get the Dirty Hunters wiped off the plant once and for all. Word would spread if we couldn't get rid of them. We'd look weak. Vulnerable. Fuckin' pathetic.

I growled low, imagining what my father, the president of the mother chapter, would say. He didn't want me to be president. He wanted Raul holding the gavel. I needed to get this shit taken care of.

The rest of the council entered: Hero, Boxer, Justin, and Lynx. Hero had breakfast pizzas in his hands as he kicked the door closed. He set out the boxes and took his seat.

I hit the gavel on the table, bringing this meeting to order. "Hendricks will do all he can to help us. Sugar and the boys will stay at the clubhouse until further notice."

"I'm sending my girl back to college early." Justin drummed his fingers on the table. "Do we have a spare prospect to send with her? I'll pay for it myself."

I raised my mug, cutting my eyes at my VP who managed the prospects. "Raul, what do you think?"

Raul considered my question. "With all the shit going on, we need to keep our most experienced here. We could send that pretty surfer dude with Emilee."

Justin growled. "Hollywood?"

Some of the guys called the prospect Hollywood because of his perfect blond hair and tanned skin. The nickname seemed to stick. *Heartthrob* might've been a better name. Not very tough for a road name, but neither was Hollywood.

Raul turned toward Justin. "He's strong and muscular but has little experience. Although, he can handle a gun well."

"You could send Ire with him. He could use the rest," Track suggested. "He won't admit it, but I know he's still recovering from his head injury."

I refilled my mug. "Yes. Send Ire with the prospect. Now, we have the run coming up next month. It's not been on my mind because of the fuckin' Hunters." I paused as some brothers dug into the food. "Hero's been on it." I nodded to my SAA. "But we need these maggots gone. We can't do the run and leave the compound vulnerable. I don't want to call in a marker for reinforcements."

Grunts came from around the table. We needed to preserve the few markers we have. Burning another one, so soon after the Fallen Soldiers helped us last month, was stupid as hell.

"I'll need a minimum of six brothers." Hero looked around the table. "But I'd prefer ten."

I reached for a slice of breakfast pizza, thinking. "What do we have, two or three weeks?" *What is wrong with me? I should know everything about the run.*

Hero scratched the top of his head, mouth full. "Not quite. Eighteen days." He drank his coffee, then cleared his throat. "The Italians don't play games up in Canada. I want to be there in sixteen days, in case we run into any problems."

"Shit." I gritted my teeth. "Continue getting the arms in order." I turned toward Justin. "If you want to get your girl out of town, do it by Thursday. We'll be moving to eighteen-hour shifts on Friday." I made eye contact with each man. "School resumes soon. I don't want my woman going back to work if the Hunters haven't been eliminated."

My brothers grunted.

"Okay, let's take care of shit." I hit the gavel on the table, ending church. "Eat up."

We powered down the food and coffee. As the room cleared out, I told Track, "I need you to stay behind."

He eyed me with a curious expression. "Yeah?"

"Let's take a ride into town." I cracked my neck, getting up. Taking this step with Angel was insanity. Never in a million years did I think I'd want to get married, but here I was, wanting to propose to my girl.

"Where to?"

I stared my best friend in the eyes. "The jewelry store."

Fuckin' Track flashed me a Colgate smile. "For what?"

"What the fuck you think, brother? You're not this stupid." *Jerk.*

"No, no, I am." The damn fool smirked. Only Track could act like an idiot with me and get away with it. "Gimme the words, brother." He laughed, fake punching me in the gut.

"You're an asshole, you know that? I want to buy my girl a diamond ring." I shook my head, leaving the room.

"About fucking time."

"Seriously?" I glanced back at him, striding out of the building. "We've only been together a little more than a month." But I was ready to legally bind myself to Madeline for life. Even after death, in the afterlife, we would remain one. Nothing could ever separate me from my Angel.

The sun hitting my face felt good. Not a cloud was in the sky. I hoped it meant good things were coming my way, like a *yes* when I asked Madeline the most important question ever.

"Yeah. For you? A week with the same woman is huge. A month? That's a lifetime."

I considered Track's words as I straddled my bike. Raising my eyes to clear blue sky, I smiled, imagining Angel's eyes. I'd known her for more than half my life—longer than everyone in the club. The twelve years apart didn't matter. She was home to me.

The way she had looked at me when she was a kid had made me feel like a king. Like I'd hung the moon for her. She still looked at me the same way. It was so damn easy to be with her. My soul could breathe when we were together. She was my safe haven, my soul mate.

I put on my sunglasses, jerking my chin to Track. "Let's hit it." I had a diamond to buy.

CHAPTER THIRTEEN

STORM

An hour later, I stalked out of the jewelers with Track—irritated as all get-out. That place was a joke. It blew my mind they were even in business with the piss-poor inventory they had. As if I'd ever give my woman a diamond smaller than one caret. Fuckin' pathetic. I told Norm, the manager of the store, he better up his game.

"It's Bastion. Nobody buys big ass diamonds in this town. We could go to the Twin Cities if you really wanna go all out. *Shit.*" Track whisper-shouted as he abruptly stopped.

I lifted my gaze.

"Well, what's this?" Deputy Miller crossed his arms over his chest. "A lowlife biker like you causing trouble in my favorite jewelry store?" He sized me up like a bitch. My hair, arms, boots. Even my crotch—the way women compared tits. This pencil dick was a loser with a capital L. "Planning a robbery or just intimidating the owner into paying you for protection."

Boiling with fury, I clenched my jaw so tight it hurt. *Stand the fuck down. He's trying to get a rise out of you.* I fisted my hands, itching to put one through the cunt's teeth. I could easily take him down. End his life. Make the world a better place. This piece of shit didn't deserve to live another day after what he did to my woman.

"Ignore him," Track gritted out.

My eyes locked on Miller's. He had a blond, porn star mustache. Since he was lean and about five inches shorter than me, I could fuckin' snap him in two—like a twig.

"What the fuck you doing in my town?" I worked to keep a level tone. The motherfucker didn't have jurisdiction in Bastion.

"Your town? That's cute." Miller snorted, strolling toward me, uniformed chest puffed out—like a big, bad deputy. Idiot. He was neither. "Just passing through."

Arrogant sonofabitch.

"Then why'd you stop?" I bit down on my back molars.

Deputy fuckin' Miller stood directly in front of me. The prick must've had a death wish. "I'm concerned about my girlfriend."

No, he didn't.

"Ex-girlfriend, motherfucker."

"Storm," Track said in a warning tone. If we weren't in public and he wasn't my best friend, my fist would be in his goddamn mouth right this second for speaking to his prez as if he were a child.

Miller tucked his thumbs in his pant's pockets. "That's right, *ex*-girlfriend. You like sloppy seconds, Storm? That's about all you deserve."

I. Will. Kill. Him.

"Gentlemen." Sheriff Hendricks appeared.

"Sheriff Hendricks, good afternoon," kiss-ass Miller said.

"There a reason you're in my town, deputy?" Hendricks cut his eyes to mine.

"I was just telling Storm I was passing through, checking stuff out because I'm worried about my *ex*-girlfriend, Madeline."

I could squeeze the air out of the prick in five seconds. Nobody would miss him. He was fuckin' taunting me. Trying to get a reaction so he could throw my ass in jail for assault. The hypocrisy of it made me sick, knowing what he'd done to Angel. The prick deserved to burn in hell.

"Get gone, Miller," I grunted, done with this bullshit.

"Not before I confirm some gossip. Is Madeline with you?"

I pursed my lips tightly together. It made me almost vomit hearing him say her name.

Hendricks stepped forward. "Not your concern, deputy."

"I care about her." Miller smirked. "Storm isn't good enough. He'll only hurt her or get her killed. Already, another gang is pissing on trees and lampposts in Winters. Marking their territory. When I stopped by Madeline's house, she wasn't there."

He went to her house? If Hendricks wasn't here, I'd snuff the fucker out and pay my time behind bars. Of course, Madeline would be furious with me for losing my cool. So maybe I wouldn't go off half-cocked. But this douchebag's days were numbered. *Numbered!*

He glared, lip curling. "I believe she's in danger with this criminal. He probably has her locked in a cell on his compound. God only knows what he's doing to her. You should really investigate, Sheriff. Women are disappearing. Being sold to the highest bidder."

I took a step, but Track moved in front of me to block me from fuckin' Miller. How in the hell did Miller know about the women? Track growled low, seething like me.

"Noted, deputy. Be on your way. I don't need any help protecting my town." Hendricks put himself between Miller and me, backing him up toward his car.

"Later, Storm. I'll check in with Madeline soon." He adjusted his crotch as if merely saying her name got him hard.

The fuck he would. I hopped on my Harley and took off without waiting for Track.

Miller would die by my hands if he went near Madeline.

I called Raul via Bluetooth.

"Storm."

"Call church! I'll be there in thirty!"

Back at the clubhouse, I was hanging by a thread. Nostrils flared, on the edge of exploding. It'd been an hour or more since I saw deputy fuckin' Miller. My heart had yet to slow to a normal rhythm. With everyone in church, I yelled about the whole damn thing. The more I shouted at my brothers, the more I thirsted for blood. The savage in me rattled the cage I'd locked him in, begging to be freed.

Throwing back my fourth shot, I shut my eyes then squeezed them tight and exhaled. Nope, I didn't feel better. Nothing would make me feel better except Miller's head on a silver platter.

"Does everyone understand my expectations?" my gaze swept across the room. Every council member was present, and so were the patched members. The room was bursting at the seams. "Miller is to go nowhere without eyes on him. At all fuckin' times!" I roared. "He's hiding something, I know he is. My mind is much too creative. It's fabricating shit left and right. I want answers!"

Grunts filled the air.

"Any questions?" I barked.

"No," shouted my brothers, like a war cry.

"Then get out there and do what needs to be fuckin' done. Get your pussy tonight motherfuckers. Come tomorrow, you won't get any more until the state is clear of Hunters." I banged the gavel and poured me another shot. "And Deputy fuckin' Miller!"

They rose their fists in the air, joining my cause. After a few moments of watching them pile out of the room, I forced a breath.

Raul had stayed behind. During the meeting, I could tell he had more to say. He wasn't a big mystery like his son, Track. Raul wore his heart on his sleeve and his thoughts were etched on his tan, leathery face.

"What?" I drummed my fingers on my glass.

"Let me call your old man, David."

"Abso-fuckin'-lutely not." I ground my teeth. Was he out of his goddamned mind? Call my dad?

Raul drew in a slow breath, then released it. "Prez, we need reinforcements."

"Then I'll call in a marker with the Soldiers."

"You already did." He pressed his lips thin as if trying to hold back his frustration.

I leveled my eyes on Raul. "This is *my* club. I said, no.'

Raul rubbed his hand along his scruffy jaw. "Yes, Prez." He sighed. "Don't let this shit with Miller steer you off track. He's just an asshole trying to get under your skin."

"He's trying to fuck with my woman."

"No, he's trying to fuck with you. So you'll make a mistake. Then he'll throw your ass in jail." He knocked his knuckles on the table. "Don't give him an inch, Storm. He might be a pussy, but he wears the badge. Don't get emotional. Believe me. I've been waiting eleven years to avenge Tina for what Gallo did to her. It hasn't been easy."

"You're a stronger man than I am."

Raul snorted, standing from his chair. "Bullshit. I'm just old and preserving my energy before I tear that motherfucker to shreds. You coming?" He jerked his head at the door.

"Naw. You go have supper. I need some quiet." I reclined in my chair.

Raul nodded and left, closing the door behind him.

Despite what he said, Raul wasn't old. The man was still hulking, just as he was when I first arrived in Minnesota twelve years ago. He and Tina had recently found out she was pregnant with their son,

Raymond when they moved onto the compound. Track wasn't thrilled about his dad having a family with another woman. This made us closer friends because I understood. My mom had a daughter, Abby, with some guy I'd never met. Abby was twenty now. Not long after she left, my dad hooked up with Jane, who was now his wife. They had two teenage daughters.

Track and I came from similar backgrounds. We both lost our moms. Only his had been murdered.

Shit. Why was I thinking about all that?

I took out my phone and stared at the picture of my Angel. My light in a dark life. My heartbeat. My soul mate. Raul had it right and I could see it now that I was focused on my woman. I acted out emotionally with Miller, letting him mess with my head.

I lifted my weary ass out of the chair. I'd have supper with Madeline and brothers, then drink a little in the bar before taking her to bed.

Tomorrow, Track and I would go into Winters to hit up another jewelry store. I was determined to propose to her. I wanted a ring on her finger by Friday.

I couldn't explain the urgency I felt. It wasn't like she wasn't mine. Something in me just wanted to give Angel her heart's desire. And that meant proposing to her properly. A wedding, then babies.

I'd do everything she wanted because tomorrow wasn't promised.

CHAPTER FOURTEEN

MADELINE

Labor Day was in a few weeks, which meant school started soon. Emilee sat beside me, tears skittering down her cheeks. We were on a bench in the back patio, my arm around her, trying to soothe her. I wasn't sure why she was so upset with her dad. He only wanted her safe. Returning to campus shouldn't be such a big deal, but it appeared to be for sweet Emilee.

"I'm just not ready to leave," she whimpered. "I was supposed to be here for two more weeks."

"I understand."

Not really, but I am trying to.

"All I know is the club is going to be busier than ever come Friday." I understood my position as Storm's ol' lady but he didn't give me many details. I did what I was told, didn't ask questions, and kept my mouth shut—meek and subservient around others. Those were unspoken expectations of my role. I respected Storm more than anyone else in my life. But me, be meek? It was so against my personality.

Keep a public face on, Maddy, I chided myself.

"You haven't even taken me to see your classroom. We haven't gone school shopping for supplies like we planned. No movies. No dining out. I hate living like a prisoner. I'm not a child!" Her tears picked up and I stroked her arm.

"Maybe we can go tomorrow. We'll do all the things we planned in one day."

Dang it. Why did I say that? Storm would probably tan my hide for not talking to him first.

She lifted her head. "Really? Do you think they'll let us go?"

Fudge. I had no clue. In bed last night, Storm was stressed to the max. When he was like that, he didn't talk. Hard fucks were all he wanted. Sex was rough and incredibly hot. He wore me plum out by the time he'd gotten what he needed.

Then this morning, he made love to me. Slow and gentle. Whispering, thank you and I love you over and over until we both came. He often did this after a rough night. It was beautiful. He told me I wouldn't see him much this weekend. Said I could invite Tara to the club for a *sleepover*. That might have been the strangest thing I'd ever heard him say. *Sleepover* sounded so weird off his lips.

When I'd arched my brow, wondering who the hell this guy was with his cock buried deep inside me, Storm said, "Shits about to get fuckin' crazy, Angel."

I'd left it at that, showered with him, and kissed him a million times before he left. My heart burned, missing him already. He'd been gone all day. They'd had church in the morning, then he left with Track for some kind of "delicate matter."

I saw him for a brief moment before Emilee and I went out back to talk. Fury rolled off him like lava down a volcano on the brink of exploding. It hurt to see him this way, but I knew it was part of his life. I'd have to get used to it. He hugged and kissed me then went to church *again*. They needed Jesus more than they needed these meetings, but I had a feeling whatever was going on would need more than a miracle.

"All I can do is ask him." I gave Emilee a gentle squeeze. "Want me to help you pack? Go over your class schedule?"

The back door opened and Dodge poked his head out. His white T-shirt, stretched taut over his braod chest and ripped biceps. The way the sun hit his golden skin made it shimmer. He was handsome with intense brown eyes and a godlike face that was nothing like his cousin Track's. As always, Dodge wore a stoic expression. His black leather cut might say Prospect but he looked like a fully patched member… dangerous and ruthless. "Everything okay out here?" His dark eyes shot from me to Emilee.

"Just girl talk," I replied with a smile.

His eyes lingered a second longer on Emilee. "Storm knows you're out here?"

I rolled my eyes. "Yes."

Dodge's gaze returned to Emilee. He gave nothing away regarding how he felt about her. For weeks I'd suspected he liked her, though. Sadly, Justin would never let his daughter date a biker.

"I'm going in to take a short nap." She leaned into me and whispered, "I'm emotionally drained."

"Absolutely. I'll see you later."

Emilee stood. "Don't forget to ask Storm about… y'know."

"I won't."

STORM

"No, Angel. Not happening." I reclined on the bed, bracing myself on my elbows.

She paced in our room, hands on her hips. Did she seriously think

I'd let her off the compound with Emilee... alone? This shit with the Hunters wasn't easy on the women. None of them liked the lockdown.

"Send a prospect with us. Or two or ten! I'm used to having someone tailing me." She rolled her eyes, shaking her head. "Or you could come with. It's just to the school. And a little shopping and maybe a movie." She bit her lip like she knew she was pushing it. Hell yeah, she was. The fact that she was asking this made my blood heat up.

"I have shit to do tomorrow." *Like, buy a big ass ring for your finger.*

"You always have shit to do. Emilee is leaving. We only have tomorrow. Can't you make an exception? Send a biker army with us, if you must. But dammit, Storm! I want off this compound." She dropped to her knees, between mine. Her hands went to my zipper, pulling it down. "Please find a way so we can go."

I inhaled a breath as her small hand gripped my cock. I wasn't controlled by my dick, but dammit, Angel knew how to make me feel fuckin' good.

"Please." Her warm tongue brushed across my slit, then swirled around my head. "Just for a few hours."

I inhaled again, burying my hand in her silky hair, fisting and tugging it. "Don't try to manipulate me, Angel. It won't end well for your ass." I looked her in the eyes.

A challenging glint sparked in her baby blues as her tongue darted out, taunting my dick.

"Careful what you wish for you," I warned, holding her gaze captive. We were so damn electric together. Fierce and determined to conquer. Combustible with a capital C.

Savage Storm and my adorable Angel. We were quite the pair. An anomaly. The Big Bad Wolf and the Easter Bunny. She was my slice of heaven on earth.

Taking me firmly in her hand, she lowered her mouth painfully slow. My heart kicked up a notch. She was so goddamn beautiful. I hated forcing her to stay on the compound. She should get to live a normal, everyday life.

Her lips ghosted around my cock. My little firecracker played me like a fiddle. Teasing me until I was close to bursting with desperate need.

I could play her game and fuckin' win.

Tugging on her hair hard, she gasped. "Suck it, Angel. I don't torment your pussy like this."

Her blue depths connected with mine. Guilt crossed through them as she realized what she was doing. "You're right. I'm sorry."

The intensity between us was indescribable. I was so fuckin' in love with this woman. Loved her with every cell in my body. She was my everything.

My thumb stroked her cheek as we stared into each other's eyes. I pushed her face toward my cock. "Suck me good, Angel."

"Will you find a way for Emilee and me?"

"Don't ruin the moment. Suck, baby." If I didn't adore this woman with each breath I took, I'd flat out tell her no. To deal with it. But I couldn't do that to her. It just wasn't in me. Hero could take the girls off the property for a few hours, along with a prospect or two. We were spread thin. Every available man was working. Even so, I'd somehow grant my girl a few hours. I'd be in Winters with Track anyway.

My eyes rolled back into my head as she sucked me into oblivion.

It should be fine. Angel would be safe, I'd make sure of it.

CHAPTER FIFTEEN

MADELINE

Storm made it happen. I was ecstatically happy and stupidly giddy to be off the compound. Hero and AJ were our bodyguards for the afternoon. Emilee was beyond thrilled to see my classroom. I was probably more excited than she was, to show off my kindergarten room.

Tara came along, wanting to drop off supplies in her room. I had a sneaky suspicion that Hero was the reason she wanted to hang out with us. Of course I'd told her he was chaperoning us. She just acted as if she didn't hear me. Silly girl. My bestie didn't fool me. She wanted Hero.

I danced my eyes around my classroom, recalling all the memories, like my kids' squeals and giggles of delight. Singing our welcome song. I could smell the paint, playdough, and dry erase markers. It'd been a great year.

Strangely, I hadn't missed any of it. Storm had me focused on him the whole summer. I wouldn't have it any other way.

"I totally love this!" Emilee exclaimed the same phrase for the third time. She was so teacher material. Flitting around the room, she "awed," fawning over the little chairs and tables, art supplies, and books. Like me, her heart was drawn to the little ones.

"Three years of college, though. It seems like I'll be in school forever." She made a pouty face.

"Nah." Tara waved her off. "You're young. It'll fly by. Enjoy the experience. Before you know it, you'll be working for a living." Tara screwed up her face. "Adulting."

"That's the truth," I agreed. "When you're in college, life is simpler. Then you graduate, get a *real* job, and suddenly you're an adult paying for everything."

Although, I liked being independent. Living with Storm, I didn't pay for anything, not even food. The commercial-grade kitchen in the clubhouse was always fully stocked. Sugar or Tina managed the grocery shopping and had an account they used to buy whatever was needed for the clubhouse. Money was never talked about, but Storm told me between all the club's legit businesses and some not so legit dealings, the KLMC did well for itself.

Couldn't say I was complaining about any of it. Well, I did have one complaint. I missed my privacy. Storm and I hadn't talked about it, but if we were going to start a family, I'd really love our own home.

"True. I'm not looking forward to adulting. Daddy says I'll never want for anything." Emilee shrugged and zoned out for a moment, leaving Tara and I hanging on her words. "Because of the club, I mean. Whatever I need, they'll make sure I have."

"Wow, so the club is like your backup, huh?" Tara crossed her arms over her chest, peering out the window at Hero. She hadn't said anything negative about Storm and his club since the party. Even after everything with Carla, Tara's opinion of outlaw bikers seemed to have changed.

Emilee paged through a Dr. Suess book. "Mhm. The club is my

family. They take care of their own."

"Think you'll find yourself a sexy biker and become an old lady?" Tara wiggled her eyebrows. More proof she had a fascination with the club.

Emilee blushed, turning away. Her golden blonde hair shimmered as sunbeams hit it near the window. "Um, probably not." She strolled along the wall of windows, keeping her back to us. "Daddy doesn't want me with a biker. He wants me to have a *normal* life, whatever that means." She sighed, gliding her finger over the globe at the end of the bookshelf. "It was Momma's dying wish that I fell in love with someone who wasn't a biker."

Oh, my heart. I needed to wrap up this conversation before I fell into a puddle of tears. Emilee was the sweetest girl. Strong too. Her momma died of breast cancer when she was in middle school. You'd never know it by looking at her. I imagined talking about her momma wasn't easy. Turning her back to us, she was probably trying to hide her emotions. I would be if it was me. Losing a mother was a devastating thought. I knew what it was to lose a brother, but losing a mom seemed even worse.

"Anyone hungry? I'm starving." I needed to change the subject before we were all crying.

Tara and Emilee turned my way with smiles on their pretty faces. "Yes!" they chimed.

"Excellent. I'm craving a burger and a Blizzard." My mouth salivated just thinking of a juicy burger. Might even go for onion rings. The KLMC compound was on the outskirts of town. Running out for fast food took over twenty minutes—one way. It'd been so long since I'd had a good burger.

"Craving?" Emilee asked with a curious expression, eyeing me weirdly.

"Yeah, it's been a while since I've been to DQ. Let's go." I clapped my hands and grabbed my phone off my desk, taking the lead out of my room so the girls would follow.

In the parking lot, Hero and AJ perked up on their bikes when they saw us.

"What's up?" Hero asked.

I stopped at his Harley. "Food. DQ."

He nodded, accepting my reply. Storm had given him strict orders to have us back at the compound by five. We were to keep to public places. He had rejected my movie idea, totally bumming me out. What I wouldn't give for a large buttered popcorn and a slurpee.

Dairy Queen was a short drive from Heritage Elementary. The girls and I sat inside to avoid the heat, taking our time eating our meal. Hero and AJ sat in the parking lot. It was sweet of them to give us space, but honestly, it was ninety-two degrees. They should've enjoyed a Blizzard in the air-conditioned dining room. Hero was more stubborn about it than Storm would've been.

Lately, I've had a larger than normal appetite. I hadn't told Storm I was a week late, nor had he noticed. Finding out our real identities, the freaking Carla fiasco, and the recent murder, I didn't want to put any more stress on him. Better to wait until I took a pregnancy test. I didn't want to get his hopes up. The emotional crap I'd been through could be the reason I was late.

"I can't believe Storm let you out of the clubhouse. It seems like since your big identity reveal, and that Carla clusterfuck, you two are even more inseparable than before." Tara snickered, popping a fry into her mouth.

She wasn't wrong. The brat was laughing because I'd overreacted and didn't trust Storm during the Carla debacle. Tara loved that I got into a catfight with the godawful woman. I should've let Storm handle her long ago. Stupidly, I tried to give Carla a chance to change. Plus, several of Storm's brothers liked her "services." The thought turned my stomach, but I didn't want to ruffle any feathers so early into becoming the prez's ol' lady. Damn, I was glad she was gone, though.

"Well, he's out with Track doing some club stuff. I have to be home like a good little girl for supper." I rolled my eyes, taking a bite of an onion ring.

Emilee nodded, dipping her fry in her chocolate shake. "Yeah, my dad reminded me about keeping my eyes open and to call him if I saw a Hunter."

"Same. Storm even mentioned Boxer giving me some self-defense lessons." I wanted to learn how to defend myself. Especially now I had a target on my back.

"Boxer is best. He taught me some moves. I doubt I could ever use them, though. I clam up, too afraid to hurt anyone." Emilee grimaced. "I guess I'm a scaredy-cat."

"Believe me, I get it," I assured her. "Never thought I could beat the crap out of anyone... then Carla happened."

Tara huffed beside me. "Well damn, you too. I'd hoped we could go to the Armory tonight. Ray's band is playing."

"The Armory? Girl, you've lost your mind. Storm would never allow me to go there without him and a dozen of his brothers." I snorted. Had she already forgotten the last time we were there, and Hunters waltzed in like they owned the place? "If my man wants me home early. I come home early."

Tara let out an exasperated sigh. "You two make me sick."

"I think they're adorable." Emilee laughed. "I've known Storm since I was six. I've never seen him so happy and relaxed. Madeline is good for him."

"Oh, I don't doubt she's good for him. It's the whole, president of a biker club and old lady shit that bugs me." She looked out the window at Hero—for like the millionth time in the past hour. "What's his story anyway?"

I followed her gaze. Of all people babysitting Emilee and me, Hero was the guy Storm gave the job to. I was sure it was beneath him, though he didn't complain. Hero's priority as SAA of the club was to protect the prez. Yet, Storm made him come with me.

"I don't know his story. Do you?" I directed my question to Emilee. Hero didn't talk much. I never even saw him with a kitten.

"I don't really know his story either. He joined a couple of years after Storm returned from the marines. He's from Los Angeles. I think he was married."

"*Was* married?" Tara stared at Emilee. "What happened? She left him or something? Did he cheat on her with a club whore?" She snorted, sipping her drink.

"He wasn't in an MC before. I think she died." Emilee made a sad face. "But I don't know the details. Tina and Sugar probably do, but I never asked."

"Wow," Tara and I said together.

Emilee stirred another fry in her shake. "Yeah, he mostly keeps to himself when he's not guarding Storm or at the gun shop."

"When did she die?" Tara's demeanor softened. Her sable-brown eyes flitted to Hero. He openly flirted with her, but she kept shutting him down. I wasn't sure why. Tara could be a mystery, even to me. We might be best friends, but I didn't know everything about her. I sensed something awful had happened when she was young. I didn't push her to tell me what, figuring she would when ready. After all this time, she still hadn't told me.

Emilee collected our garbage. "One time, I'd overheard Tina saying Hero ran away from LA after his wife died with no plans of returning."

"Damn, that's rough." Tara didn't take her eyes off Hero.

This conversation depressed me. My heart went out to Hero. If he ran away, something horrible must've happened. I imagined it'd take a lot for a big, ferocious man like him to leave all he knew.

"Hey, maybe we could get our nails done." I steered the topic away from Hero. Something in my gut told me he wouldn't appreciate us talking about him and his wife.

"I'm free." Tara shrugged. "Got nowhere to be and no one to go home to."

Damn, I felt like the worst bestie ever.

"Me too. Nowhere to be." Emilee's warm honey-colored eyes locked on mine. "But will Storm let us?"

Excellent question.

The roar of motorcycles made my heart lurch. Emilee appeared to have the same reaction, turning to look out the window. Hero and AJ jumped off their bikes.

"What's going on?" Tara asked.

"Motorcycles," Emilee replied.

Tara leaned into me to see. "So? I don't get it."

My heart thumped a little harder in my chest when Hero lifted his phone to his ear. Was he calling Storm?

"Hunters are still in the area causing trouble." I grabbed my phone. If Storm called, I'd know it was because of the possibility of danger.

Three bikers slowed as they passed the restaurant. They weren't Knights; they were Hunters. My stomach twisted as I held my breath. They didn't slow down or stop as they craned their necks checking out the parking lot. Maybe I was just hyper-paranoid after the recent murder. But something didn't feel right. I squeezed my phone, watching it like a ticking time bomb. My heart raced, anticipating Storm's face appearing on the screen. He'd call immediately if something was up.

"Dang, talk about a tense moment. Let's get out of here and go to the nail salon." Tara rose from her seat. "I think you both are too uptight."

I glanced at Emilee. We held each other's gaze a long beat, then shrugged. Maybe we were uptight. Storm had drilled into my head that the easiest way for the enemy to get to him was through me. I didn't take his warning lightly. I'd seen what happened to Ava and Nancy.

I knew about the murdered college student. Tara was oblivious. I couldn't tell her about any of it, per Storm's orders.

When I chose to be with Storm, I accepted the risks. Not that I wanted to be in danger. I just wanted to be with him more than I feared for my life.

I smiled, thinking of my man, *Kaleb*. I loved calling him by his given name when we were alone, but I also loved his road name, Storm.

Storm sounded powerful and dangerous, which my man was both. Kaleb, well, he was my one true love. Ink-free and adorable back in the day. Roll the two into one, and I had a magnificent man.

My heart fluttered, thinking of him as we strolled out to my car. I pulled up the contacts on my phone for the nail salon Tara and I went for pedicures. It wasn't easy to do with the afternoon sun glaring down on us.

"What's up?" Hero stalked toward me.

I lifted my eyes to his. "We wanted to get our nails done. You okay with that? Sit inside an air-conditioned building."

A pained expression crossed Hero's face. "Your nails?" He wiped sweat off his brow.

"Yeah. They give massages there. Maybe you can get one." I smiled wide, hoping to entice him. If he rejected the idea, Tara would probably have a fit.

"Not really feeling a massage…" he mumbled.

"What? Bikers don't get back rubs? Too cool for that, are you?" Tara pushed her hip out, resting her hands on it. She was giving him an attitude, just as I thought she would.

"Roja, I'll agree if you sit on my lap and rub against me." He winked, sporting a shit-eating grin. With her, he never skipped a beat.

"You wish!" She made a gagging face.

AJ, Emilee, and I laughed, while I found the phone number.

"Storm won't go for it, Angel." Despite joking around seconds ago, Hero was back to his serious self. "He wants you home for supper."

"Honestly, it won't be long, an hour maybe," Tara said before I could answer. "Let the prisoner have a little fun."

Okay, prisoner? Not cool, Tara. I was exactly where I wanted to be with the man I loved. Gah, she could be such a brat when she wanted.

"It's not safe, Roja. Let me try Storm again." Hero turned toward me. "Did you see the bikers pass?"

"Yes." I fiddled with my phone. "What do you mean call Storm *again*?" Something felt off. Was Storm not answering his phone? That wasn't like him.

"I got voicemail a few minutes ago. Then I called Raul. He said to bring you and Emilee home once you were done eating. Only Storm can overrule him." He put his phone to his ear. "I didn't tell you right away because I didn't want you to worry. But he's not called or texted me back."

Guilt crashed over me. I shouldn't have suggested getting our nails done. What if Storm wasn't alright?

Tara looked disappointed. Emilee appeared off since the Hunters rode by.

There we were like a gaggle of teenagers in the parking lot. Distracted by my stupid nail suggestion. Hero grumbled about Storm still not answering. Emilee's eyes darted around as if waiting for something to happen. AJ seemed to be keeping an eye out, too, while Tara went on about me being a prisoner.

Why did I mention our freaking nails?

The sound of screeching tires and the smell of burning rubber made me whip my head to the side. A white van with blacked-out windows barreled toward me. I screamed, thinking it was going to hit me, but it didn't. Thank God, it stopped.

"Run inside!" Hero yelled, drawing his gun.

I hesitated, confused by what was going on. It was just a minivan.

The side door flung open. Three men wearing masks jumped out. Hero charged toward them. One grabbed me from behind and I screamed. He shoved a rag into my mouth. I shook my head, struggling to break free as I searched for Emilee and Tara. Did they run inside?

"Stupid bitch, you're coming with us," the man hissed in my ear. "Get the others!"

Everything felt like a dream… A painfully slow nightmare. The masked men were dressed in black. As I watched from the sideline, I only heard the whooshing sound of my pulse. Nails dug into my arm, dragging me back. I couldn't get any traction wearing flip flops. If I'd had my boots on, I could kick and stomp on his foot. Instead, my sorry excuse for shoes came off as I tried to pull away.

AJ ran toward me, drawing his gun. *Yes! He'll save me.*

An arm went around my neck, putting me in a chokehold. My attacker let loose of one of my arms. I couldn't tell what he was doing. Needing to get away, I kicked at the dude's shins while gagging and clawing at his arm.

Mere feet from me, panic flashed in AJ's eyes just as gunfire ensured. My ears rang, knocking me off balance. AJ dropped to the ground, eyes wide. Blood poured from his chest, soaking his shirt. Bullets flew. I wasn't sure where they were coming from. I stared at AJ, tears streaming down my face.

No! God, no! AJ! I tried to scream but only choked on the rag in my mouth, unable to break away. He was bleeding too much. I needed to stop it. He needed me. *God, help him. Please…*

I searched for the others. A masked man hit Hero over the head with a lead pipe. He went down hard. My heart seized. Both of our bodyguards were injured.

Emilee ran toward the entrance door. She was tackled to the ground.

Tears flooded my eyes as I fought the man holding me. How could I suggest lunch? A stupid manicure?

Storm… I needed him desperately.

Dragged halfway inside the van, Tara leapt onto the back of the man. She hit him over and over. I couldn't hear her yelling through the ringing in my ears. Hero was unconscious on the ground, getting kicked in the gut.

It happened so fast. What was a fun afternoon with my friends turned into a nightmare.

I couldn't scream. Couldn't breathe. Tara was elbowed in the stomach and fell to the ground. Emilee was tossed into the van with me, Hero next. Tara fought until she was knocked out by the butt end of the gun.

I felt so helpless, sobbing like a baby. Why wasn't anyone helping us?

"You stupid bitch. You're more trouble than you're worth," the man gritted out, slamming the door closed.

Everything faded as my Storm's handsome face flashed in my head.

I'm so sorry…

CHAPTER SIXTEEN

STORM

I slowed on my Harley as another pang hit my chest. The sons of a bitches came and went at the oddest times. It was strange. I was only thirty so it couldn't be my heart. Could it? *Damn, I have no idea. Maybe I should have Patch check me out.* I hadn't had a physical since I was in the Marines.

It couldn't be stress-related either. Madeline and I were better than ever. I even suspected she might be pregnant. I felt it down in the marrow of my bones. My Angel *was* pregnant with my baby. I could tell by the changes in her body. Though I hadn't mentioned it on the off chance I was wrong. Her dusky mauve nipples were darker. Little green veins appeared on her tits. Sugar told me she'd been taking naps in the afternoon while I was out. It was possible none of those were signs of pregnancy, but I hoped my woman was having my baby.

Madeline deserved an engagement ring. She wanted a wedding. I'd give her whatever her heart desired. Because my woman was my rock, the calming balm to my chaotic spirit, my everything. I guessed all that might be the culprit for these sharp little pains. I was about to have everything I wanted—my woman as my wife *and* a baby. Life was beautiful. Maybe my heart was having trouble adjusting to this change of pace.

Track slowed to a stop on the dirt road leading to the compound. I pulled over to the side as he took a phone call. He waved his hand, telling me to go. Another pang hit me, this time in the heart.

"Go, go, go!" he yelled, taking off like a bat out of hell.

Shit, something had happened. The pain in my chest grew. Maybe I was having heart issues after all. I'd call Patch after dealing with whatever was amiss.

Track and I pulled through the open gate. Dodge was out front, like he'd been waiting for us. Madeline's parking spot was empty. Fuckin' hell. I'd told her to be home by five.

It was after five-thirty.

I inhaled a deep breath, forcing myself to not blow a gasket. Pushing my kickstand out, I got off my Harley, irritated as fuck.

Track cut me a sidelong glance. "Let's go but stay cool, man."

Right. After Madeline disobeyed me. Not happening. She was lucky I let her off the goddamned property. Fuck, my firecracker knew how to rile me up.

Track ran into the clubhouse. Why was he running? What the fuck was going on?

"Who called?" My blood pressure rose with every step. Something felt off. Was I about to have a heart attack? I pressed my chest, wishing to ease the pain.

He rushed around the building, without so much as an answer.

"The fact that you're telling me to stay cool is proof you know it's bullshit Madeline isn't home." I clenched my jaw, blasting through the glass door. I needed a drink before calling my woman and giving her a major ass-chewing.

Track looked over his shoulder at me. He didn't seem right. Still hadn't answered me.

"What's going on?" I would kick Hero's ass when I saw him. He knew better than to defy my orders.

"Where the hell have you been?" Lynx made a beeline toward Track and I. "I've called you a dozen times and sent just as many texts!"

"Excuse me?" I stopped, narrowing my eyes at Lynx. I didn't take kindly to being yelled at. I was the fuckin' president. This boy needed to show some respect.

"With Track. Don't you ever yell at me like that again!" I passed him, then stopped, wholly taken aback by the grave air in the bar. "What the fuck's going on?" I grabbed a beer from the fridge. "Somebody die?" I twisted the cap off the bottle.

"It's a Madeline," Lynx said.

I whirled around to face him and removed my phone from my pocket. Another sharp pain sprouted in my heart. "Shit! I forgot to turn it back on after the jew..." I mumbled the last part of the word because nobody knew about the jewelry store. Track was the only one. "What about her? If shit went down like the last time I was gone, I'm gonna bust some faces!"

"Christ, I wish it was just that." Lynx gripped the back of his neck.

"If it was so important, why didn't anyone call Track?" I gritted my teeth.

Lynx threw his hands up. "I didn't know he was with you! Because I'm a fucking idiot!"

"Clearly!"

"The Hunters..." Lynx's voice trailed.

I checked my call log and saw Lynx's number several times, then checked the texts. There was one from Madeline.

The tension radiating off Track put me more on edge. He hovered as if knowing I'd lose my shit.

"What about the little maggots?" I opened the message, trepidation building in my stomach. Another pang in my chest hit me like a Mack truck.

Angel: Hello prez. Got your pretty lady with me. Can't decide what I'll do with her tight little body. Keep her or sell her to the highest bidder. Got her friends too. And your SAA. I'll be in touch – DH.

My hands trembled as the greatest fear I'd ever felt roared through my body with tsunami strength. The message had been sent over an hour ago. My whole body violently spasmed. *My Angel...*

"Goddammit!" A guttural roar ripped from my throat as I let out the beast I kept locked up. I threw my beer at the mirror behind the bar. I swept my arm across the shelf. Dozens of bottles fell and shattered on the ground as I continued to cry out in agony. "Nooo!"

"Prez, I... I..." Lynx stuttered.

Track took my phone out of my hand as Raul entered the bar.

"The Hunters have my woman!" I yelled to anyone listening. "Call Justin! Those fuckers have Emilee too. And Hero! Fuck and AJ. Get every available brother here!" I barked orders like a crazy man. "I want everyone on the streets! Now! They have my woman!"

"Jesus Christ," Track said in a venomous tone.

"I already have men in Winters." Raul gripped my bicep. "Pull yourself together."

"Anyone touches her, I will kill them! Kill them!" My chest burned as I tried to draw in oxygen. I couldn't breathe. Fuck, I couldn't fill my lungs. Dread ripped through my body like a deadly F5 tornado.

Raul squeezed my arm. "Calm down, son. Wolf and Jill saw squad cars and an ambulance at Dairy Queen." Raul swallowed. "They saw Madeline's Honda in the parking lot and went to check it out. AJ is gone."

I cut my eyes to his. "Gone? What do you mean?" But I knew. Fuck, I knew.

"Dead."

I grabbed the back of my neck. "Jesus," I hissed.

"The Hunters won't hurt them if they think they can use them for leverage." Raul put his hand on my back.

"Storm." Sugar slipped into my side, wrapping me in a hug. "She'll be okay."

I felt on the verge of breaking, but I couldn't. I had to keep my head.

"You put the tracking app on Madeline's phone, didn't you?" Track asked.

I nodded while he clicked around on my phone.

"Shit, it looks like her phone is at DQ. I'll call Wolf." Track stepped to the side.

My heart thundered so hard it felt like it was going to burst out of my chest. If those fuckers hurt any of them, I would destroy every single one of them. If they laid even a finger on my Madeline, all hell would break loose.

"Here, Prez. Take the edge off." Lynx handed me a tumbler of whiskey. "I'm sorry about this."

"No," I snapped, tossing back the amber liquid. The burn did nothing to ease my nerves. "This is my fault. I shouldn't have let her leave. I knew the Dirty Hunters were pissed at us, wanting revenge for us plucking off their men."

"Hey." Track appeared from behind me. "Wolf said Madeline's phone was in her car. Prospects are bringing it back. Wolf's bringing Hero's bike."

"Good."

"She's gonna be okay. She's strong." Sugar whispered, still holding onto me.

"I'll never forgive myself if something happens to her. The Hunters are a bunch of animals. Goddammit!" I squeezed my eyes shut and tilted my head up. I didn't want to imagine what the bastards were doing.

Track growled. "We'll destroy the whole fucking lot of them."

"No mercy..." I shouted as we parted ways. "I'll be in my office." I needed a moment to rage in private. I could depend on Raul and Track to get shit in order. I just need a minute.

"Where's Storm?" A loud growly voice yelled. "Storm!"

"Who's yelling for me?" I stopped, turning around.

Dodge appeared, chest heaving and hands fisted. He looked ready to kill.

"What do you want?" I barked at him.

"I need to talk to you and Track."

"Gonna have to wait." I continued down the hallway.

"Now, goddammit! We talk now!"

I turned on my heel, sneering. "Excuse me, motherfucker?"

"In private," Dodge demanded.

"Boy, you are lucky you're Track's cousin, or I would beat your face into a bloody pulp." I was barely hanging on by a thread.

Dodge exhaled a labored breath. "It's important... about Emilee."

I grabbed Dodge by the arm and jerked him to the side, and hollered for Track. Dodge's breathing was about as erratic as mine. We stared at each other, waiting for Track.

"What?" Track entered the hallway. When he saw his cousin in my grasp, he scowled. "What's going on?"

"Your cousin here has important information about Emilee. He wanted to talk to you and me." I bore my gaze into Dodge.

Track crossed his arms over his chest. "Spill it, Danny."

"Dodge," he hissed.

"Boy, say what you gotta say, or I'll beat your ass myself." Track got in his cousin's face. "I don't have time for your punk-ass shit."

"Emilee is my girl," Dodge blurted.

"Come again?" Track shoved him in the chest.

Dodge squared his shoulders as if ready to fight. "You heard me, Emilee is *my* girl. I need to help find her."

"You will be where I say you'll be, *prospect*," I cut in. Who did this punk-ass kid think he was?

Dodge faced me. "No Prez, she's carrying my baby. I need to help find her… them."

Track scrubbed his hand over his cheek. "Jesus, Mary, and Joseph. You have got to be kidding me." He slapped Dodge upside the head. "If her dad finds out, no one will be able to save your ass. Not even the prez here."

Dodge stood firm against us. "I don't need saving, cuz. I need to find my woman."

"She ain't a woman. She's a girl. A nineteen-year-old girl, and you got her pregnant?" Track pinched the bridge of his nose. "Justin is going to kill you. Then chop you in pieces and feed your worthless ass to the fish."

"Enough," I shouted through gritted teeth. "I don't have the patience for this drama. You can stay," I told Dodge. "But you better listen to the orders because if you screw up and endanger *my* woman, I'll cut your balls off and shove them up your ass. You get me?"

"Yeah, Prez. I get you."

"How far along is she?" I asked, unsure if I wanted to know. But it made me think about Madeline. Dammit. My stomach tightened.

Dodge's face softened a little. "Just found out before the barbecue. Five weeks."

"Sonofabitch," Track hissed. "What was it, a one-night stand?"

Dodge blanched, clearly offended. "Fuck no. We've been together since Christmas. Just been hiding it."

"Christ," I rasped. "Boy, get out of my face." I pushed him away.

"Okay, Prez." He fell back, heading for the bar.

"I'm sorry about this." Track paced. "I sponsored the little shit. I can't believe he knocked up Justin's only daughter. You don't need this crap right now."

I shook my head, hands on my hips. "Justin's going to lose it as it is with his daughter missing. Her being pregnant will send him over the edge. You better find a way to keep *Danny* out of his way."

"I will. Wolf should be here soon. I'm going to go talk to my dad."

"Church in thirty," I told him.

"I'll be there."

I returned to the bar for another shot. Lynx must've read my mind, pouring me a glass. I nodded, then swirled the amber liquid before tossing it back. I welcomed the burn in my throat, trying to focus on it, but all I saw as I squeezed my eyes shut was Angel's face.

Fuckin' Hunters. We should've driven them out of the state a long time ago. We should've made a statement, challenged them, and showed them we wouldn't take their shit.

"Storm?"

I turned toward the hesitant voice. "Jill."

"I… um, found this notebook in Madeline's car. When I went to put it back, this note fell out." She handed me a paper. "I only glanced at it when I saw your name. I wasn't sure if it was important."

Wolf stepped up behind Jill and wrapped his arms around his trembling old lady. "Prez, I talked to one of the deputies. Lots of gunfire was reported. AJ had one shot to the heart. He's been taken to the coroner."

I held the paper in my hand, barely hearing Wolf's words. "Okay." I stalked to my office, closed the door, and went to my chair.

My hands shook as I unfolded the letter.

Kaleb, my love,
I have a weird feeling something awful is going to happen. You

weren't here when I arrived to ease my fears. On the off-chance I never see you again, I wrote you this letter. God, I hope I'm just overreacting, but I feel it in my bones. Something horrible is coming.

Whatever you're thinking about Tommy's death, stop. JUST. STOP. It was an accident, baby. I know it was. I don't blame you. Toby told me everything. I want you to know, none of it changes the way I feel about you. I still want to be with you. I want to be with you more than anything. Every day I dream about us having a baby and our future together. A life with you is all I want.

I love you, Kaleb Knight. I have since I was a little girl. I will love you until I draw my last breath. Whatever happens today, tomorrow, or years from now, never stop living. Even if I'm gone, keep moving forward.

Yours always and forever,
Angel

I stared at her words, her handwriting. She must have written it the day she caught Carla in our room. Madeline had sensed something was off. She was so damn perceptive. Always. But the part about drawing her last breath undid me. I leaned over my desk, crossing my arms on it, and put my head down. And I broke into a sob.

This was all my fault.

If I didn't get Madeline back in one piece, I'd pull the roof down around me. I'd personally hunt down every fuckin' Hunter and do to them what they did to her.

When I get you back, I'll marry you and never let you out of my sight again.

CHAPTER SEVENTEEN

MADELINE

I couldn't stop shaking as I fought back my tears. *Don't show weakness. Stay strong.* I couldn't be sure, but it seemed we'd been missing a couple of hours. No question, Storm was out of his mind with worry. Why didn't I listen to him and stay on the compound? So stupid. It was my fault we were here. My fault my man was sick with worry. My fault AJ was hurt… or worse.

My muscles tightened in my shoulders, remembering the single gunshot. Swallowing my emotions, I refused to believe what I knew in my heart to be true. AJ wasn't dead. He had to be alive.

But there was so much blood pouring out of his chest. He'd gone white as a sheet as he stared at me.

No, AJ's okay. He's got to be.

I tilted my chin down, glancing at Emilee. When I'd woken up in this unknown place after they captured us, it overwhelmed me. Panic had flooded my veins. Emilee and I were alone. Filled with terror. No sign of Hero and Tara in this metal building.

God, please, let them be okay.

Maybe they were left behind. Maybe they ran to get help?
Everything happened so fast. My brain could've fabricated them being
in the van. Everything was so fuzzy I couldn't make sense of it. I
hoped that was the case, then they could get to Storm. The club would
rescue us.

Yes, they're getting help. Help is coming.

I forced myself to breathe through my mouth. The rank-smelling
air made me nauseous. My skin crawled as I kept an eye out for the
mice I saw scurrying around.

My heart rate hadn't normalized since I woke. I was hot and dirty.
Throat, bone dry. Scared for our lives.

"I need to tell you something," Emilee whispered so quietly I
barely heard her.

Our fingers entwined as we sat huddled together against a filthy
metal wall. I guessed we were inside an empty grain silo, judging
by its cylinder shape and tall ceiling. They were everywhere on the
outskirts of town. Never had been inside one, until now. They looked
bigger from the road.

"Mhm." I flicked my eyes toward the guard, hoping he didn't
notice us whispering.

"You know Danny?"

Danny? The name didn't sound familiar. Had she mentioned him
during one of our conversations, and I missed it? Emilee didn't have
any friends in Bastion. Justin kept her on a tight leash. It surprised me
that he let her go away to college. Emilee had told me that he felt she
was safer a few hours away from the MC.

"No. I don't know Danny." I kept my voice low. The Dirty
Hunters prospect had no problem slapping us around. My aching
cheekbone was proof. I'd gotten a little mouthy when we first
arrived. Storm would be furious that I didn't keep silent. After getting
backhanded, I heard my man's voice telling me to shut it and not anger

anyone. I'd been quiet since. Our safety was my top priority.

"I mean, Dodge, he guards the gate at the compound." Emilee snuggled closer into my shoulder.

"Oh, yeah. Nice guy." *Oh my gosh. She's talking about Track's cousin. Her father will lose it.* Alarms went off inside me as I sensed she was about to drop a bomb.

A tear skittered down Emilee's cheek. "He's so nice. We've been dating in secret since Christmas." She squeezed my hand.

There it was, a ginormous confession.

I wasn't surprised Dodge liked Emilee. She was a beautiful girl. Sweet and personable with long hair the color of spun gold and warm, honey-colored eyes. A natural beauty. Wholesome. I wondered how she was interested in Dodge. He hardly talked and wore a constant scowl. Similar to the other guys in the club, he was rough around the edges. Like he'd seen some shit in his life.

I never thought Emilee would be with him, knowing how her parents felt about bikers. On the same thought, Dodge was ballsy for getting with Emilee. Justin had made his position regarding his girl and bikers abundantly clear.

Storm flashed in my head. People probably said the same thing about my intimidating man and me. We were an unlikely pair. Who knew a tattooed, tempestuous biker and a kindergarten teacher would be perfect together—an ideal match. The same could be true for Emilee and Dodge.

Emilee squeezed my hand, pulling me back to the present.

"Wow… In secret, huh?" For nearly nine months! How did they hide it so long?

"My dad will have a cow when he finds out."

I gave her a slight nod. "Mhm." I completely understood. Even though I loved Storm, life at the compound wasn't pleasant. I understood why her dad wanted her out of the MC life. I had a feeling Emilee felt as I did. I loved Storm more than the danger I was in. It wouldn't keep me from being with him.

My stomach churned, imagining Storm's reaction when he found out I was missing. Emilee squeezed my hand twice. I'd zoned out again. She whispered, "I'm pregnant."

My head whipped toward her, mouth gaping.

Another tear rolled down her sweaty, red cheek. "Five weeks."

Oh shit...

I tucked her into my side, my heart hammering erratically as a protective, maternal instinct flooded me. Emilee's body trembled, her tears picking up.

I faintly recalled the Hunter's enforcer saying they would auction us off. It was right after I'd come to. *Did I imagine it? Dream it? Maybe he only wanted to scare us.*

What if they weren't intimidating us with empty threats? If we weren't rescued, would they really sell a pregnant young woman? What about me?

Acid shot into my throat as my hand went to my stomach. I never got a chance to buy a pregnancy test. Did I need to? I swallowed. No. I knew I was pregnant.

My mind raced. Maybe I could convince them to let Emilee go. She was so young and innocent. Sheltered most of her life. Had lost her mom. I couldn't sit by and let them hurt her.

Though my life wasn't so different from Emilee's, I preferred them to keep me and release her.

But then, I didn't want to be sold either. Why would they listen to my plea? My stomach roiled.

"Storm and his men will find us before anything bad happens," Emilee told me, as if she knew I needed assurances. "But we've been here for a long time. What's taking them so long?" Just like that, her confidence faltered.

"I don't know."

We were in a grain silo somewhere. How would the Knights

ever find us? I didn't have my cell phone with the tracking app. We probably would've been rescued already, had the Hunters not left it in my car.

I dropped my forehead onto my bent knees. *I did this to us...* I should've never left the compound. Storm didn't want me to, said it wasn't safe, but I'd begged. Tempted him with my mouth.

Then I called Tara to join us on a girls' day out. I put us in this situation.

Justin would blame me for his daughter's abduction. Hell, the whole club would blame me. Probably Storm too.

Hot tears blurred my vision. *Don't fall apart. Be strong for Emilee.*

Somehow, I needed to get us out of here in one piece. I wrapped my arms around Emilee, holding her close. I'd do whatever necessary to protect her. I owed it to her and Justin after putting her into this dangerous situation.

My eyes drifted closed. It hadn't been long when they flew open at the sound of a loud booming voice.

"Let's get this show started!" a man entered through the only door into this metal container. "Where are my lovely ladies?"

Emilee and I stiffened beneath his gaze. Behind him, two men followed, dragging Hero between them. I gasped, holding my breath. Hero's face was busted up and bleeding.

My heart seized as I choked back a sob when Tara was brought in next, her bare feet scraping along the ground. Why wasn't she fighting? Why wasn't she looking at us? There was blood on her shirt. Neither moved, their heads hanging as if unconscious. What had they done to them?

"Over there, Prez," the young prospect said.

"Shut your fucking mouth. We don't want them to know who we are. Think, boy!" The prez slapped the prospect upside the head. He was an idiot if he thought it was hard to tell who ran the show.

Emilee flinched, squeezing my hand.

"Stay calm," I whispered, though I had a hard time holding it together.

The short, stocky prez strutted our way. My heart jackhammered as he eyed me.

"Here's how this is going to play out. If Storm complies with my terms, you'll all be set free. If not, I'll either sell you or keep you for myself." He laughed, a vile expression on his face. "Which one is his ol' lady?"

"None of us," I said on a snort, trying to bait and throw him off his game. If he believed they captured the wrong woman, maybe he'd let us go. Maybe.

The prez shook his head. I blinked just long enough to miss the back of his hand flying my way. Emilee cried out, squeezing my right hand when he made contact with my face. I grunted, trying to absorb the urge to sob.

"Motherfucker," Hero yelled, but it was weak. The men holding him flung him to the ground. He was punched in the gut, multiple times. Tara whimpered, but I couldn't make out her words. At least she was alive.

I licked the blood on my lip, cupping my left cheek where the prez struck me. I couldn't let this situation escalate. Whatever it took to keep us all safe, I would do it.

"Listen to me, bitch. Lie or smart off again, and I'll make you sorry. I promise, you won't like your punishment," he hissed in my face. My gag reflex hit, smelling his putrid breath. Had he eaten a shit sandwich? "Understand?"

I nodded, fighting the urge to cover my nose with my hand.

"Good girl." He glowered at me. "Now I know you're the ol' lady. Been keeping an eye out for you. Just waiting for the perfect opportunity to snatch you."

I nodded to appease him. My only concern was protecting Hero,

Tara, and Emilee. And her baby, of course. If I could keep all the attention on me, that would help.

"I'll be calling your ol' man in five. He knows I'm calling. He'll want to see his woman in one piece." He jerked his head to Emilee. "Who does she belong to?"

"Nobody. She's my friend." I lied, hoping he'd lose interest in her. He couldn't find out she was a council member's daughter.

"Oh, well." He shrugged. "Least I got the prez's woman, his queen. He'll do anything to get you back."

I shook my head emphatically.

He got in my face, sneering. "What? Why you shakin' your head?"

"He's the president. I'm not important to him. Not long ago, I caught a club whore in our bedroom. The bitch said she was waiting for round five with him."

His eyebrows shot up. "The fucker's got some stamina."

"Don't be impressed. The asshole betrayed me. I won't put up with that shit and don't want his pathetic ass anymore." I hated myself for saying that, but I do anything to get us out of this alive.

"A tough broad, are you?" His tongue swept over his bottom lip.

I shrugged my shoulders, trying to not let his lecherous grin get to me.

"I see the fire in you, baby. There are a lot of men who like a feisty woman, a fighter. I bet you're not submissive, are you?" He hissed, licking his lips.

"No, I guess I'm not." My skin prickled. *Jesus, help me.*

His smile widened, showing off two silver teeth. "Get undressed. Down to your bra and panties."

I stared at him, holding my breath. He was serious.

"Her too." He jerked his chin toward Emilee. "Gotta show the goods."

"Oh, God…" Emilee whimpered.

"Leave her out this… please. She's young. I'm all you need."

He narrowed his eyes as I stood and unzipped my shorts and wiggled out of them. The hungry look on his face disgusted me. I removed my blouse to keep his attention off Emilee.

The prez licked his chops. "Only one way to get her out of taking her clothes off." He stepped in front of me. His foul breath… I'd hurl any second if he didn't back the fuck up.

"How?" My stomach flip-flopped, fearing his condition.

"Strip for the camera when your ol' man is on the phone."

"No, Madeline. Don't," Emilee cried out. "I'll take my clothes off."

"Shh!" I snapped—stupid girl. Didn't she know I was trying to save her? I swallowed, working to keep calm. "I'll do it."

"That's what I like to hear. Miss Tough Biker Babe, taking one for the team. All right, when I tell you to strip, you better do it, or else she'll pay." He pointed to Emilee.

"I will." What other choice did I have? This man didn't give a shit about Emilee or me. He wanted Winters Township and would do anything to get it. I had no desire to find out how far he'd go to get it.

"No, Madeline…" Emilee quietly sobbed into her hands.

I tried not to sob right along with her. My heart broke for Emilee. She was only trying to protect me as I was her. But I couldn't let her experience abject humiliation in front of these disgusting pigs or the Knights. There was no question in my mind Storm's brothers would watch with him. Saving Emilee was the right thing to do, but in doing so, I had no clue what it would do to me.

It wasn't like I was that much older than nineteen-year-old Emilee. I was only twenty-three. I'd already been abused and didn't want to know what it felt like coming from them.

I was the reason any of us were in this mess. I needed to do everything possible to keep us safe and unharmed.

Even if it meant losing a piece of myself in the process. Dane had broken me before. I prayed I could handle it again.

CHAPTER EIGHTEEN
STORM

Out of my mind didn't come close to how undone I felt. I sat in my trashed office, seething. Why the hell I had anything in here other than a desk and chair was beyond me. These Hunters had enraged me so much the last couple of months, my office looked nothing like it had before they rolled into my territory.

Everyone left me alone to get control of my emotions, but fuckin' hell, it wasn't happening. My woman, my brother, and two more women were taken. AJ… dammit, AJ was dead.

How the fuck was I supposed to calm down after what these bastards had done?

And my Angel. Christ Almighty, I couldn't stop thinking of the dead woman found raped and beaten in the forest. I buried my face in my hands as emotion clogged my throat and burned my eyes. *If anything happens to Madeline…*

I dropped my gaze to her letter. The only piece of her I had in this office. I heard her sweet voice reading to me. Felt her soft touch soothing me. Smelled her shampoo. Tasted her... goddamn, I needed her so fuckin' much.

A double knock at the door had me lifting my head.

"Storm, everyone's present for church," Track said through the door.

I checked the time. Shit. The Hunter's president would be calling soon, according to his text.

My chest tightened as I tried to inhale a breath. Not happening. "Be there in a minute." I barely got the words out.

I would've been out searching with the others if the message hadn't come. I was afraid to imagine why he'd want a live streaming video. Raising myself out of the chair, I tried to inhale a deep breath to no avail.

Whatever I did, I couldn't look weak in front of my brothers. No matter what, I set the example. I was their prez.

When I entered the room, the tension floating in the air raked down my spine, piercing my soul. The weight of their grave expressions intensified my anxiousness over this dire situation.

I cleared my throat. "In five minutes, the president of the Dirty Hunters will call." I paused to still myself. My fucking heart raced so damn fast. "I don't know what he'll say. What he'll do. Or what his conditions will be, aside from wanting Winters Township. Stay silent."

Grunts filled the room.

"I mean it." I made eye contact with Justin. He gave a slight nod. Like me, he was barely holding it together—wanting to make those dirty fuckers pay. I scanned the table. "No outbursts. You could put Hero and the girls in more danger than they're already in."

"Yes, Prez," they called from around the table.

I drew in a shallow breath, the muscles in my shoulders and neck coiled tightly, fear rushing through my veins. I turned to Grizzly. "Ready?"

He nodded as the 75-inch flat-screen on the wall came to life. I stared at it emotionless, to hide how terrified I was. The waiting was killing me. I needed my woman back unharmed. I needed her to be okay.

Drumming my fingers on the table, time ticked by excruciatingly slow. Each second increased the strength of a booming storm building inside me. Hurricane strength destruction would land soon. The only thing to temper the savage in me was Madeline. My Angel. She better be in one piece and okay.

My Angel...

The phone rang. I cut my eyes at Grizzly, then Track on my right and Raul on my left.

Inhaling a pathetic, calming breath, I answered gruffly, "Storm speaking."

"Prez. Let's skip the pleasantries." The smug sonofabitch snorted as I stared at the black screen. "I have your woman, as you know. *Mujer Hermosa.*"

"What the fuck you say?"

"I said, beautiful woman, *estúpido*. That means stupid." The asshole snorted. "Didn't you take Spanish in school, *ese*?"

I could choke this motherfucker for baiting me. Soon he'd find out what a bad idea it was.

"You're wasting my time, asshole," I grunted. Why hadn't he come on the screen? What was his game?

"Oh, really? Well, your woman says she's pissed at you. Caught a club whore in your bedroom. Tsk, tsk." He snorted again. "What kind of fool are you cheating on a gorgeous woman like her?"

My blood boiled as he taunted, but I knew those were Madeline's words. Why would she bring that up? She knew it was a hoax. Carla lied. I'd proved I didn't betray her.

"What do you care?" I gritted my teeth. "Let me talk to my woman."

"Too bad for you, *ese*. She doesn't want you anymore. It's rather advantageous for me."

"It doesn't matter what she says. She belongs to me. I. Own. Her." I growled, tightening my hands into fists. Yeah, I sounded like a fuckin' caveman. But this asshole understood the ways of an MC. Women were viewed as property, nothing more.

Madeline is fuckin' mine.

"Yeah, figured you'd say that. Women always think they call the shots. In this case, it may be true. I've negotiated with your woman."

"Come again, asshole? You don't fuckin' negotiate shit with my woman!" What the fuck had Madeline agreed to? Or was this cunt screwing with me? He couldn't be stupid enough to hurt… or kill her. I'd feel it in my soul if she was gone. My Angel was alive. Because I was so sure, I would spank her ass when I got her back for sticking her nose where it didn't belong.

"*Ese*, your woman's convincing. I'm sure you know this."

Damn straight, I knew what Madeline was capable of. Just the thought of it pissed me off even more.

"You see, I told her and the girl to undress down their bra and panties. But your woman had another idea." The asshole laughed as if he'd just heard the funniest joke in the world.

Justin gripped the edge of the table, hands shaking. I shook my head, a silent warning to calm the fuck down. It was hypocritical, given the fact that I didn't know if *I* could calm the fuck down. A mental picture of Madeline taking her clothes off for those bastards made me murderous.

"And? Continue, goddammit," I ordered. Shit was about to get ugly.

"And… your woman is taking one for the team. She's worried about the girl, Emilee. Said she'd do whatever I said so her friend didn't have to take her clothes off."

Fuck! I bit the inside of my cheek until I drew blood. "That fuckin' isn't happening! I want to talk to my goddamn woman!"

"Oh, I'll do better than that. Live feed coming your way…"

I watched the flat-screen. My hand shook, holding the phone while I squeezed my other fisted one tighter.

"Storm…" Madeline suddenly appeared. Fuck, she was in her bra and panties—but it wasn't so bad, just like a bikini on the beach—I tried to tell myself.

"You okay, Angel?"

She bobbed her head, keeping it down to avoid looking directly into the camera.

"Head up!" the asshole yelled.

When she lifted her chin, white-hot fury shot into my chest like a bolt of lightning. I clenched my jaw. They'd hit her. More than once. Those motherfuckers were finished.

"Talk to me, Angel. I need to hear your voice."

"I don't want to talk to you. You cheated on me for the last time. Four times may not be much for you, but I'm done."

What the fuck? Cheating four times? I flicked my gaze to Track. He shrugged. She had to be trying to tell me something.

"Four isn't much, babe," I said like it wasn't a big deal.

"Really? What if I was with four men?" Was she trying to hint as to how many were with her?

"Ha! Presidents don't like to share, bitch." The Hunter prick laughed.

I ignored him. "Baby…"

"Don't baby me." Her shoulders shook. "I'm not in the mood for your shit. I'm hot, thirsty, and my allergies are acting up, so fuck you, Storm!"

Jesus, her words stabbed me in the heart. She didn't mean it. I'd keep telling myself that she was trying to get a message to me. Yeah. She loved me.

The Hunter laughed again, but the fool didn't know she was trying to help us. Madeline didn't have allergies.

I played along. "Hay fever does it to you every year, makes you grouchy."

"Shows how much you know, asshole... it's grains, not hay."

I cut my eyes to Grizzly. He nodded his head rapidly, tapping away on his laptop.

"None of this would've happened if you'd stayed home instead of pigging out on burgers and Blizzards." Ouch. I may have taken it too far.

She gasped, appearing hurt by my words. It only took her a second to recover. "Shut up! I went out for comfort food with my girlfriends while you were fucking a kitten!"

"Enough!" The Hunter's prez was back. "I'm tired of your lover's quarrel. You ready for the show, Storm? I sure am."

Show? Was he going to kill her in front of me? I stood from my chair. Track grabbed my wrist. I glared at him, but I knew he was trying to help me stay in control.

"What show?" I did my best to hide the fear in my voice.

"Your woman's going to strip for us. It was part of the deal we made, so the other girl kept her clothes on. Your woman needs to take it *all* off."

I faintly heard angry grunting in the background. When Madeline turned her head, I knew it had to be Hero. He was with her, but it sounded like he was gagged and restrained.

"Fuck, no! She better not!" I was about to have a heart attack. Sweat beaded on my forehead, my pulse thumping in my ears, chest squeezing like a vice.

The fucker laughed. "You don't really get a say, Prez."

"I'll kill you if you touch her. What the fuck do you want?"

"I won't touch her if you move out of Winters and agree to a truce. You stay out of my territory. I'll stay out of yours." He was full of shit.

"Winters is my territory! Look at a fuckin' map. Draw a line from the center of Bastion out forty miles and make a circle. Everything within it is mine. Winters included."

"Well, I want Winters. If you don't agree, I'll sell the women to the highest bidder. I might keep one, but I can't decide between the girl or your woman." His fingers glided down Madeline's arm. She jerked away as I bit down on my molars, nearly cracking them. "Or that redhead, but she's too much of a fighter for my taste. Already had to show her who's boss."

What'd the fuck did that mean?

"It'd take too much to break her in, but I know plenty of men would enjoy the challenge. They like a woman who fights back."

Shit. It sounded like he had hurt Madeline's best friend.

"Don't do it, Storm," Madeline yelled. "Just find these assholes and take them down. Avenge me!"

She did not fuckin' say that.

"Shut up, bitch!" The motherfucker backhanded her. And again. Madeline's head went back, bobbing like a doll. I clawed my nails into the wooden table in front of me.

"I told you to keep your smartass mouth shut!" A third fuckin' time, he hit her.

Madeline didn't cry as blood dripped from her mouth. Goddamn, I hurt for my sweet Angel.

"Storm. I know this is a big decision. Your woman or your territory, so I'm giving you thirty-six hours to decide. After that, I'm putting the women on the dark web." He pulled Madeline's hair, forcing her head back, and kissed her neck.

I will kill him.

"Take it off, *Mujer,*" he ordered through gritted teeth. "That means *woman* if you forgot, Storm."

I shook my head, fisting my hands. Glaring at my brothers seated at the table, they all turned toward me, taking their eyes off Madeline. When they hung their heads out of respect for her, I nearly broke.

I couldn't breathe as rage rushed through my veins and tears welled behind my eyes. My pulse whooshed violently in my ears, watching Angel take her bra off, then panties.

I heard Emilee sobbing and Hero going nuts in the background, but Madeline remained calm as her lip trembled, eyes glossy. Her tears didn't fall. She wouldn't let them. Those pricks couldn't break her, but I knew she was dying inside. There wasn't a fuckin' thing I could do to save her.

"Fuck, Storm! Your woman is perfect." He ogled her like a hungry animal. "Lucky sonofabitch. Look at these perky tits. I just need a little squeeze, babe." He touched her, fuckin' pinched her nipple, making her wince!

I'll cut off his goddamn hands.

"Hairless pussy too. Damn, bet she's good eats, huh, Storm? Men will want to know. What about her mouth? Does she give good head? Is she a good fuck?"

"You motherfucker!" I roared, slamming my fists on the table. "I'll castrate you and pull your innards out through your mouth! Keep your fuckin' hands off her!"

"Only one way to assure that, Storm. Give me Winters." His fingers raked down Madeline's arm again.

Madeline shook her head, a defiant glare in her eyes. The bastard cupped her pussy hard, and she yelped.

"I'm coming for you, you sonofabitch! I'm coming for you!" I yelled, seeing red, heart dying for my Angel. "I'm going to kill you with my bare hands!"

"Say goodbye to your woman, Storm. Thirty-six hours…" The flatscreen went black, terminating our connection.

I knocked over my chair with the back of my legs. Whirling around, I punched the wall over and over as a primal roar ripped from my lungs. I bloodied up my hands, not giving a fuck. My woman was just groped and humiliated by that motherfucker.

I. Will. Kill. Him.

I was so goddamn out of my mind angry. Nothing would ever calm me until I had Madeline in my arms, safe and in one piece.

"We're going to find her. Every man in this room is determined to find her," Track said in a low, lethal voice.

Grunts echoed in the room.

"What she did for Emilee ..." Justin choked up, squeezing his eyes shut. He opened them and they were wet. His afflicted gaze locked on mine. "Jesus, Storm. I..." He hung his head, lip trembling.

"I know." I capped his shoulder, then headed for the door. "I need time with the punching bag. Boxer..." I shouted over my shoulder to my enforcer. I needed to blow off steam in the gym out back. Not that I believed it would help, but I had to do something to clear my head. How was I to put a plan together to bring Madeline and the others home if I couldn't think straight?

Madeline needed me clear-headed and not losing my shit. I needed to regroup after what just happened to her.

My sweet Angel. I wouldn't rest until she was safely back in my arms and every one of those motherfuckin' Hunters was six feet under.

CHAPTER NINETEEN

STORM

A dozen of my brothers were out scouring area farms by one in the morning. The council and I had stayed behind to study the video. I wouldn't have been worth shit on my bike. Too much adrenaline rushed through my veins.

I'd deleted the part where Madeline was forced to strip. Each time I thought of it, remembering the agony and tears in her eyes, I raged like a savage. Readying to tear the Hunters' prez to shreds. Then I'd think about my woman, tap down my unhinged emotions, and focus on finding her and the others.

What we knew for sure, they were in a metal building. The way Angel talked about allergies, Raul suggested we check out grain silos in the area. It was something, and we ran with it.

The part where she said I cheated four times and asked how I'd feel if she were with four men had to be a clue. We agreed there must've been four Hunters with her.

My girl was damn smart. Quick on her feet.

We needed to be.

Hour after torturous hour, my girl occupied my every thought as we put a plan together. Now in my office, I rocked in my chair, sometime after eight in the morning. My eyes were closed after my sixth cup of strong, black coffee. I'd had a monster migraine since the video call.

I sensed someone standing in the doorway. I'd left it open to hear the activity inside the building. Didn't want to miss anything.

"What?" I grunted.

"Thought you were asleep." Track's voice was low.

"Asleep while rocking my chair? Asleep while my brothers work their asses off to find Madeline and the others? Asleep while God knows what's happening to my woman? Fuck no, I'm not asleep." I stopped my chair, opening my eyes, shooting a deadly glare at my best friend.

"Clearly not." Track dropped into the chair in front of my desk. "A grouchy cuss like you needs some rest… at least a nap. Go up to your room. I'll wake you in a couple of hours or if I hear something."

"No."

"She'd want you to rest."

"No!" I slammed my hand on the desk. It was fortunate my mug was out of the way, or I would've knocked it over. "You saying you'd sleep if your woman was missing?"

"Point made. But a nap will help."

"I'll nap here… later."

"Storm your bed—"

"I can't," I said through gritted teeth. "I'll smell her in the bed, brother. I can't…" I rubbed my hands over my cheeks, utterly drained, not having slept in twenty-four hours.

"Shit, man." He scratched the back of his head. "I get it. This shit has got to be ripping you up inside."

I grunted. Track had no idea how fucked up I was. I couldn't show my true feelings, couldn't look weak to my brothers. I was dying. Fuckin' dying. Sick with worry for Madeline and the others. Grieving the loss of AJ. It was all too much.

A paralyzing fear seeped into my veins when I'd nodded off an hour ago. I'd had the worst nightmare of my life. Those goddamned Hunters, one by one, had their way with my Angel. Her blood-curdling screams had jolted me awake.

"Do you need anything?" Track leaned forward, resting his elbows on his thighs.

"Just my woman."

"Right. Well, I'm gonna check in with my dad. He was calling in a marker."

"I don't want him using them up. We may need them for Brynne." Brynne was Tina's daughter who was attending college in Montana. We had two sets of eyes on her at all times. Just waiting for the day when we'd capture her and reunite her with Tina. Raul may need his markers for his old lady's daughter.

"Don't worry about Brynne. We gotta get Madeline and the others back. They're the club's immediate priority." Just hearing him say Angel was a priority helped me breathe a little easier. My brothers wouldn't rest until she was found. Hearing it comforted me.

"Thanks."

Track nodded and left.

I pinched the bridge of my nose, clenching my back molars and fighting the sting of tears. *She's strong, a fighter. She'll come back to me.*

Grabbing my mug, I went to the kitchen. Sugar and Tina stopped in their tracks when I entered. The whole room fell silent, eyes on me. Likely waiting to see what I might do. All morning I'd gone off like the short fuse they knew me to be. I didn't give two fucks about it. My woman was missing. I couldn't be responsible for my actions in the mental state I was in.

"What can I get you, honey?" Sugar took the cup from my hand.

"Just coffee."

She filled the mug, a nervous twitch in the corner of her lip. "You need to eat."

"Can't."

She frowned, handing me the cup.

As Tina approached, I recognized the determined glint in her eyes. "Hey, you'll find her—all of them. Madeline would want you to eat. If you crash and burn, how can you take care of her? She's going to need you, Storm. Gotta keep up your strength. Now sit so I can get you some breakfast." Tina jerked her head to a stool.

I obeyed, bracing my elbows on the island, dragging my hand across my face.

"How do you do that? You're like the stubborn-biker whisperer." Sugar scrunched her nose and winked, placing her hand on my shoulder.

Tina shrugged with a wry smile. "I just have the magic touch, I guess."

Sugar leaned in and whispered, "Call David."

Ah, that was why she had a nervous twitch. "No."

"Storm, he has more manpower." Her voice was low, so no one else heard. She knew how to be discreet. She also knew asking me to call my dad was risky. The mere fact she mentioned him had me studying her face with narrowed eyes. Something felt off.

"Don't need his help."

David Knight, the president of the mother chapter in South Dakota, was the last person I wanted to call. After what happened with Tommy, he'd thought of me as a blundering dumbfuck. My failure at keeping my woman safe would only prove him right.

"It shouldn't matter what you want. What matters is bringing Angel home in one piece." She huffed, leaving me in the kitchen. Dammit. I didn't need Sugar angry with me on top of everything else.

"She's right, y'know." Tina patted my arm, setting a plate in front of me. Great, she heard Sugar. "Eat."

"I've got this." I pushed the plate away from me, my stomach roiling. Did I really believe I had everything under control?

Tina cocked her head, crossing her arms over her chest. "I'm going to tell Angel what a pain you were while she was gone. Then I'm going to sit back and enjoy the show when she hands you your ass."

I snorted, actually snorted, wanting nothing more than my woman handing me my ass. Hell, I'd even let her do it in front of my brothers if it meant getting her back. My chest burned, imagining her fired up. My little brunette firecracker wasn't always docile. Fire and brimstone flowed through her just like it did me. Only she controlled it better.

"She's going to come back to you. Eat the toast, at least. She'll need you to be alert to her needs."

"My Angel can count on me," I replied in a harsh tone. No one should ever question my abilities to take care of my woman. Maybe they weren't sure I would because I didn't keep her safe. My gut twisted, forcing me to grip it.

Tina placed her hand on my shoulder. The understanding in her eyes made me ill. "This isn't your fault."

I glared at her, standing from the stool. "The fuck it isn't."

"Storm—"

"No!" My eyes darted around the kitchen. A few brothers and kittens were watching me, but I didn't care. "Don't tell me this situation isn't my fuckin' fault! I should've gotten the Hunters out of the state months ago. If my woman and the others aren't returned in one piece… if I have to bury my…" The agonizing thought bent me over at the waist. Excruciating pain wrapped its clutches around me to the point I couldn't stand.

Tina put her hand on my back. "Slow breaths."

Breathing was more painful than my knotted gut.

"Hey. Let's go." Track nudged me out. Boxer and Lynx were at the door.

"I'm sorry," came Tina's sad voice.

"It's okay," Track told her.

"Get him to eat," Tina whisper-shouted from behind me.

Track didn't respond.

We went out of the clubhouse. I paced like a trapped lion, gripping the hair on the top of my head. I felt out of control. Helpless. On my last nerve.

"Where is my woman?" I roared, pulling my hair. "Any fuckin' thing could've happened to her. She could be out of the state. The fuckin' country by now. Jesus..." I dropped to my knees, gasping for air. If she was out of the country, it could be impossible to find her. But I wouldn't ever stop searching. Hoping. Loving her.

A guttural scream tore from my lungs as I dug my nails into my head. Curling into myself, I rocked, unloading everything that had been building inside me. I let it all out: anger, fear, hate. The hate I felt for myself was almost as horrendous as the fear I had for my Angel.

My brothers surrounded me, placing their hands on my back and shoulders to keep me anchored. Protecting me in this weak moment. They didn't feed me lies or give me false hope. This situation could end only two ways, depending on what we did about Winters Township. Their silence told me they understood the state I was in. And they were here for me.

We were family—a brotherhood like no other.

We weren't like some clubs who chanted *brothers before others*. We didn't subscribe to that way of thinking. My Uncle Matt showed me how his old lady, Sugar, and their children meant the world to him. He expected the rest of us to have the same mindset. Still, my brothers and I would go to the ends of the earth for each other. Take a bullet if it meant saving the other, like AJ. We would always have each other's back and our old lady's and children, like Justin's daughter.

Minutes passed before I'd gotten my shit together. A hand gripped each of my biceps, lifting me off the ground. A flask was thrust into my hand. It didn't matter if it was morning; I needed it to settle my nerves. I took a swig, embracing the burn.

"We got you," Track muttered in a lethal tone. I was sure he hated seeing me this way, just as I would feel about him. Seeing a brother breakdown rarely happened. When it did, it crushed us all.

"Got two things to tell you. I need you stable." Boxer squeezed my arm.

I lifted my gaze, meeting his deadly ice-blue orbs. "Tell me."

He looked at Track, who nodded.

"First, my contact in Winter's Sheriff's Office said Miller has been on edge the last few days. Last weekend, he was seen talking to a couple of Hunters."

I fisted one hand and took another swig from the flask. "What else?"

Boxer gripped my bicep as if he sensed my inner turmoil. After serving in the Marines together, he read me well. "Miller ducked out of work today saying he wasn't feeling well. I'm expecting an update within the hour."

I stared Boxer in the eyes. "He's mine even if his involvement is small." I cut my eyes to Track and Lynx. "You hear me? Miller is mine. That fucker who made my woman strip and assaulted her, mine too. They. Are. Mine."

"The Hunter's prez we can't promise," Track said.

I seethed at his words. "Why the fuck not?"

Track squared his shoulders. "Raul called in a marker after the video call."

My chest squeezed tight, feeling anger and *gratitude*. Raul might've needed it to bring Tina's daughter home. Instead, he burned it for me. I owed him big. This was a debit I didn't know if I would ever be able to repay, but I would damn sure try.

"Why didn't anyone tell me sooner?" Going behind my back was never acceptable. "And why isn't he telling me himself?"

Track sighed. "He's out riding with the others. You were messed up, man. He didn't know if anything would pan out. Didn't want to give you false hope."

"I'll deal with Raul later." I rubbed my eyes with the tips of my fingers, feeling the grit caused by lack of sleep. It was also too damn bright out. "What did he find out?"

"He called just before I pulled you out of the kitchen. Turns out the Dirty Hunters are from California. Their prez's name is Dawg. He was part of another MC, Westside Heretics."

I crossed my arms over my chest. "I've heard of the Heretics. Big into selling blow and prostitution. They occupy Northern California."

"Well, Dawg tried to take out the Heretic's president. The dude is in a coma." Track shook his head.

My brows shot up. "No shit?" Trying to take out your president was the ultimate betrayal.

Lynx laughed, lighting up a smoke. "Stupid shit."

"He's a wanted man." Track cut his eyes to mine. "The prez's brother, Miguel Avila, is his VP. He's been after Dawg for months. The second that Miguel heard he was in our territory from Raul's contact, he got on a private jet. He and some of his brothers will be here soon. They plan to clean out the Dirty Hunters in the area."

I stared at Track, feeling like we might have a chance. A bit of hope sparked, dead center in my chest. My Angel could be back before the end of the day. Within hours, hopefully.

Sugar ran out of the clubhouse. "Storm! Oh, God."

The panic on my aunt's face made my mood take a nosedive. I stalked toward her. "What's wrong?"

"Um…"

The rumble of motorcycles stole my attention as they stopped at the gate to my compound.

"Who the fuck is that?" Boxer pulled his gun.

Track and Lynx followed, drawing theirs.

I tensed, taking a few steps forward. We weren't expecting anyone. It sure as hell wouldn't be the Hunters. Dodge approached the bikers, rifle in his hands, ready to defend. Narrowing my eyes because the damn sun was too bright, a weird sensation hit me. I knew the man in front.

Sugar stepped in front of me. "I didn't think he would come so fast."

He?

I knew exactly who she meant. "You called David?"

"I'm sorry." Her eyes teared up. "I called him after the video call."

"What the fuck do you know about the call?" I cut my eyes to Track. Raul must've told Tina and she filled Sugar in. "Sonofabitch."

"You can deal with me later. I would do anything to bring Madeline home safely, even reach out to David… behind your back. I only wanted to put him on standby, hoping you'd call him yourself. It's why I had nudged you to do it earlier. I guess he'd taken matters into his own hands."

"Fuck, Sugar. You know I'd never ask him for help!" My phone buzzed in my pocket. "Yeah?"

"Prez, it's—" Dodge hesitated.

"I know who it is. Let them in."

"K, prez."

Sugar got in front of me. "David said he knew you'd never ask for his help when I was on the phone with him. A few minutes ago."

"A few minutes ago?" I was stunned.

"Yeah, he wanted to announce his arrival. I'm sorry." A tear rolled down her face. "I'm just as shocked as you. I never expected him to come all this way without your permission. I'm so sorry."

I bit the inside of my cheek until it bled. I was furious. Two people I trusted went behind my back. "Get in the clubhouse, Sugar. Get the kittens to help you and Tina cook. Looks like we're going to be feeding a dozen more people."

Between my dad and his brothers, and the Heretics, we'd have a full house. I didn't need this shit on top of everything else. But I would swallow my pride. *Today I'd do anything* to bring my woman and the others home.

"Here, eat this damn piece of toast so Tina will get off my ass." Track shoved it into my hand with a wry grin. "Angel will be home before the day is over. I feel it in my bones."

"Fuck yeah, brother. Send those vibes my way." I bit the toast in half.

My old man rode toward me. I didn't hate him. But I sure as hell didn't like him after the way he treated my mom and me. David Knight was a selfish bastard. He only cared about his club and himself. He believed in *brothers before others*. I was just an *other* to him.

Now, he was here at my club.

He strode toward me, not waiting for anyone. Some things never changed. He removed his shades and tucked them into his vest pocket.

"Prez," I grunted, standing boot to boot with my father.

"Storm. Before we get started, I want a word in private." His stormy gray eyes bore into mine. "Take me to your office." It wasn't a request. He turned on his heel and led the way into *my* clubhouse. Because he was the National President of Knight's Legion MC, I didn't have any other choice but to do as he said.

"Stay cool," Track whispered as I passed.

Everyone watched us in awe. Seeing us together wasn't a common sight. Even when attending the annual Knight's Legion event, I avoided my dad at all costs.

From the back, he looked like Uncle Matt. My chest tightened, wishing he were here instead of my old man.

Dad had his phone to his ear. "Jane, we made it. I'll call you tonight after we get Storm's woman back."

Christ, the confidence in his voice had my chest practically caving in on my heart. How was it that a grown man could feel reduced to a snotty-nosed kid in front of his father? This was why he was the national president. He was all swagger and arrogance, never believing he couldn't do what he set his mind to do.

I was like him on a smaller scale. More hotheaded and stubborn too. But there was no doubt in my mind he had his own agenda.

What the fuck was he *really* doing here?

CHAPTER TWENTY

STORM

"Yeah, baby. I will." David grunted, ending the call as he entered my office. I half expected him to drop into my chair as if it were his, but he didn't. Instead, he shocked the hell out of me, throwing his arms around me in a giant bear hug after I kicked the door shut.

"Missed the shit out of you, son."

What the hell? My body went ramrod straight. The last hug I could remember my dad giving me was the day my mom left. I was nine, crying my eyes out as he held me, whispering, *We don't need that bitch.* But my old man didn't know shit. I had needed my mom.

I sucked in a breath as he squeezed me. My mind whirled like a funnel cloud of confusion and nausea pummeled my gut. But I also couldn't shove him back.

"Wish I'd known about your woman before now. Sugar said, you call her Angel. I like it. Can't wait to meet her." He released me and we stared at each other for a long beat.

Who in the hell was this man? An imposter, replacing the father I knew. Maybe he was on some fucked up meth and trippin' like he used to when I was a kid.

"Who are you, and what the fuck did you do with my asshole father?" There were at least a dozen other names I'd prefer to call him. Since he was here to help find Madeline, I'd show him a speck of respect.

He smirked, slapping me on the shoulder. "Still a Grade-A smartass."

"I learned it from my old man."

"Least you learned something from me." He sat in the chair in front of my desk. "Take a seat." He jerked his chin to my executive chair.

My mind raced as I eyed him. After all the stress of dealing with Madeline missing, I felt like my defenses were down. I couldn't deal with my dad being, what? Fatherly? It was throwing me off. We weren't like *this*.

"Jane sends her love and prayers for you and Angel." He rubbed his hand over his scruffy chin. He never had a beard. By the smell of it, he still wore Brut aftershave. Deep creases were etched into his forehead. His brow was always furrowed. At fifty-five, he was physically fit with salt and pepper hair. He was still a badass motherfucker.

"Thanks." I had to be in another universe.

As Angel would say, *mercy*. Jane sends her love? Prayers? They were never religious.

"Gotta say, you're freaking me the fuck out. Why are you acting like we're close?"

"Always brutally honest. Don't you ever get tired of being so blunt?"

I considered him as he stared back at me. Same stormy gray eyes as mine. What was his game?

"No."

David sighed, relaxing in the chair with his arms crossed over his chest. "We don't have time to waste talking about us. I just want you to know you can trust me in getting your girl back. You can depend on me, Kaleb."

Dammit, he used my birth name. He hadn't said it once since he made me leave home. Before I had a road name, he only called me *boy*.

"Think you deserve to be trusted and relied on?"

He hiked an eyebrow. "From your point of view, probably not. From Jane's and your sisters—"

"Half sisters." I squirmed in my chair, not wanting to go down this road.

He growled low. "They're my daughters. That makes them your sisters."

"I don't even know them."

"That's gonna change." He leaned forward in his chair. "I want my son back."

I fought the urge to storm out of my office. This wasn't the time to deal with family shit.

"Don't wanna deal with this now. My woman is my priority." I inhaled a shallow breath. "You're here to help. I appreciate it."

He rubbed his hands on the tops of his thighs. "You're right. Angel's well-being is the number one priority."

I grunted.

His gaze met mine. "Some of your cousins will be here anytime from North Dakota. Abe, Micah, and Jonah."

I blinked, utterly shocked. He called in reinforcements for my woman? And the others?

My dad's cousin, Ben, was the president of the North Dakota chapter. Minnesota was mine. Last few years, Dad and Ben had been working on planting another chapter in Montana. One of Ben's sons would hold the gavel. My old man wanted the Knights to occupy the northern states to make it easier running arms to the Italian Mafia up in Canada.

"I don't know what to say. Thanks, I guess."

"Don't need to say anything. I should've come sooner. I knew you were struggling to get the Dirty Hunters out of Minnesota."

I snorted. Of course, he knew.

He shrugged. "I'm glad Sugar called. Last thing I want is for you to lose your woman." He stood, a small curl to his lip. "We need more Knights, y'know. To carry on Grandpa's legacy."

"Well, after getting taken, Madeline may want nothing to do with the club. Or me." I rubbed my chest, right over my heart. That pain in my chest was as strong as ever. *Could this be the event that makes her leave me?*

"Nah. I doubt it. From what Sugar said, she's strong and madly in love with you. She's in it for the long haul. She'll be bringing you little ones lickety-split."

I hoped he was right.

"I can't think about the future or kids right now. Saving and avenging Angel is all I'm capable of right now." I stood from my chair and went around the desk.

"Then let's do it." He put his hand out to shake. I accepted with a grateful smile.

I'm coming for you, Angel. We're all coming for you.

CHAPTER TWENTY-ONE

STORM

After our private meeting, we gathered in the quiet bar. Conversations were dialed down. The air was full of smoke. Hell, even I toked on a joint to calm my nerves—something I didn't do often—like when I was in my early twenties.

Plans were hatched to turn the area upside down. My dad didn't know my territory, so he sat and listened. It was strange. I tried to focus, but it was hard not to wonder what he was planning. Selfish sonofabitch probably had some debt in mind that he'd make me repay for this help.

Sugar entered, making a beeline for me with three towering men following her—my cousins. David and I stood at the same time.

"Storm, I'm sorry about your girl." Abe embraced me in a brotherly hug. His road name was Cobra. We used to raise hell together when we were young, along with his brother Micah—Bone, who was VP in their dad's club. Haven't seen much of them since we grew up. "We'll get her back, cuz."

"Cobra, I appreciate you coming." I pulled back, turning toward Bone and Buff, and hugged them.

Cousin Ben's family were aviation enthusiasts. Every one of them had their pilot's license. They flew around the country and into Canada for their club's business, predominantly drugs and guns. Ben's five sons' road names were after airplane types. His only daughter, the youngest in the family, was named Piper.

"Spectre wished he could come." Bone gripped my bicep. "But you know how it is, Dad needed his Sergeant at Arms to stay close."

I understood completely, now that my SAA was gone. "Having the three of you here means a lot."

The bar was filled with my family, yet I felt utterly empty without Madeline and Hero here. Sugar and her boys were talking with Cobra and Buff. David and Bone were with Justin. This group of brothers was the best. I was damn grateful for them.

Boxer stalked toward me with a hardened gaze. "I got her!"

The room fell silent. I held my breath.

"Tell us," I barked, heart racing with anticipation.

Boxer climbed on a chair, Mr. Dramatic, and yelled, "I have the location of where the Hunters are hiding. I believe that's where the others are too." Boxer cut his eyes to mine. "Get your kevlar on and load up. I'll be in the arms room waiting for you." Boxer hopped down.

"Are you sure this farm is where my woman's at?" I gripped the back of my neck, wanting to believe him.

David and Justin stepped up beside me.

Boxer nodded, his laser ice-blue eyes showed his certainty. "Pretty damn sure. My informant followed the Hunter after he met with Miller. His gut told him to follow the dirty maggot and it paid off. Led him straight to the farm. He's not left the location and has seen three Hunters go into one of two silos."

"Fuck." I put my arm around Justin. "Let's get our girls back."

As everyone scrambled to get ready, Track showed up with four others.

"Storm, this is Miguel," Track introduced.

"Sorry we're late." Miguel shook my hand, looking around the room. "What's happening?"

I smiled at Track. "Boxer's informant got us the location of a farm he's seen Hunters in and out of."

Track shook my shoulder. "Hell yeah, brother."

"We need to roll." I cut my eyes to Miguel's. "Do you and your brothers need anything? Kevlar vests, guns?"

"Nah, man. We're ready." Miguel patted his chest and flashed his weapons.

"I'll drive them out in my truck," Track said.

I nodded. "All right. Let's do this."

My council faced the rest of our brothers in the bar with the Heretics. My cousins, Maddox and Markey, were also present. I'd given them permission to attend the meeting if Sugar said it was okay. They were only observers and would not join in the rescue.

Not everyone was going to the farm. It'd look like a fuckin' army of bikers if they did.

Instead, we'd have men strategically placed if any Hunter tried to escape. I did something unprecedented: I called Sheriff Hendricks because the farm was in his jurisdiction.

Here at the clubhouse, Sugar and Tina cooked up a feast with the kittens. Patch, the club's doctor, was here setting up his medical room. Libby, a kitten, was helping him. She had her nursing assistant's degree, but liked being a kitten more. Any time she helped Patch, she got a hefty bonus.

"You have your orders. Follow them," Raul yelled, explaining how everything would go down. "If you fuck up this plan, Boxer will fuck you up. You hear?"

Grunts came from every direction.

"If you catch a Hunter, bring him here. Grizz," he pointed to the corner where Grizz had his iPad with him, "he will tell you what to do with him. Listen to your leader. And leaders, follow the orders I gave you!"

"All right," I shouted. "I'm counting on you to do this as quietly and inconspicuously as possible. We don't shit where we eat, motherfuckers. Watch out for the locals. I don't want any innocents caught in the crossfire. Hear me?"

Yeahs were yelled.

"Be safe. See you back here when this shit is over." I hit the gavel on the table and watched them file out. I hoped to God we didn't have any more casualties. I swallowed, flicking my eyes up as I thought of AJ. No time for grieving. We had four lives to save.

I'm coming baby, just hang on a little longer. I can't live without you, Angel.

CHAPTER TWENTY-TWO

MADELINE

Emotional exhaustion won the fight. I wasn't sure what time sleep had taken me, but eventually, I'd nodded off. The prospect watching us left after his replacement arrived. It must've been hours ago when the men switched places. When the door opened, the sun streamed in, blinding light brightening the inside of the silo. I was willing to bet it was late morning or almost noon.

Worry consumed me from the inside out. Every little noise set my heart racing as I feared for Emilee, Tara, and Hero's safety. Each time I dozed off, I dreamed of AJ getting shot. The sound of the gun going off was so vivid I'd jolt awake, drenched in sweat and gasping for air. I'd looked at my hands, relief washing over me. They were only dirty. In the dream, they were covered in blood. I wasn't sure if he was dead or alive, but I was sure all this was my fault. God, I prayed AJ was okay.

I felt an enormous amount of guilt. Shouldered the responsibility. It tore me apart, imagining what Storm must've been going through. What I put him through.

I'm so sorry... so sorry.

Terror fed on my soul at what these monsters might do to us. The way they watched Emilee and me made my skin crawl. But I couldn't show weakness, my fears. I just couldn't, for my own sanity. Letting them break me, like Dane had, might annihilate me.

Each time I cracked an eye open, the new pervy prospect was staring at me. He creeped me out more than the last one.

Time dragged on at a snail's pace. Maybe it was good. Maybe bad. I didn't have a clue one way or the other. The longer we were in here, the worse it might get for us. I doubted after last night's show, the prez would keep his hands off me. A shudder of disgust shot through me.

Emilee was asleep, leaning against my shoulder. Poor thing tried to stay awake, so I wasn't up by myself, but she couldn't keep her eyes open. I couldn't blame her. She was growing a tiny human in her tummy.

Then again, I was too.

She shifted in her spot, groaning quietly. "I have a splitting headache," she murmured.

I patted her hand, which was still in mine, shushing her. My head hurt too. We were dehydrated. The prospect last night only gave us one bottle of water to share. I'd let Emilee drink most of it. That was hours ago. Before, I was forced to undress for the camera.

"I'm sorry, hon." God, I was so incredibly sorry.

"You both awake?" The prospect strutted over. His jeans hung low on his hips, his black t-shirt had a hole in the armpit. He looked Latino with dark hair slicked back, tan skin like the enforcer. Maybe they were related. "The boss wants you ready for him. He'll be here in a little while." He tossed a couple sticks of gum at us. "He wants your breath minty fresh."

I stared at the gum, trying to read in between the lines. Why did the prez want our breath fresh? *Dammit.* I knew exactly why.

"Can we please have some water?" I asked as nicely as I could stomach. "We're grimy too. Is there a bathroom we could use?" I was probably pushing my luck, but we'd never know what they'd let us do if we didn't ask.

"You don't need to be clean for what the boss will do to you." He laughed wickedly. It struck holy terror in me, the likes I'd never felt before. "But I'll grab you both a bottle of water if you'll give me head. That red bucket over there is your toilet." He jerked his chin to the side.

"No," I blurted without hesitation regarding his disgusting request. A blow job? He might as well kill me now.

"I'm just bullshitting you." The prospect left.

I exhaled a shuddered breath of relief. But I was sure I might not be so lucky the next time I said no.

Last night flashed in my head like a horror flick. I couldn't see Storm during the call. I only heard him and knew he could see me. I imagined a grim, disgusted, and enraged expression on his beautiful face. Fury pulsing through his veins, murderous thoughts pummeling his mind. And all for me. His silky baritone voice soothed my frightened soul when he called me Angel.

I had every faith in Storm, my cunning, ruthless, outlaw biker. He wouldn't stop until he found us. I only hoped it was before one of us got hurt, like Tara and Hero.

Each time Hero mouthed off to one of the Hunters, they beat the shit out of him. For the time being, they were only using their fists and feet. I had a feeling they'd eventually get tired of Hero. I didn't want to imagine what they might do.

And Tara?

Tara had been gagged since they brought her into the silo. I was sure she'd run her mouth off, so they shut her up. The Hunter's prez sniffed around her a lot, touching her red hair, whispering into her ear. Tara and Hero were at the opposite end of the structure. I couldn't hear what was said, but I could see Tara trembling and rage building in Hero each time someone went near her, laid a finger on her.

Emilee whimpered. "What are they going to do to us?"

Poor girl, looking to me for answers I didn't have. After what the prez did to me last night, I honestly didn't want to imagine what he'd do next. Especially if Storm didn't give him Winters.

I couldn't imagine the Knights and Hunters in the same area. The Hunter's prez couldn't honestly believe Storm would simply hand Winters over. Let them live here without making them pay for what they did to me. I heard it in Storm's voice when he said he'd kill the prez with his bare hands. He'd do it. Frankly, I wanted him to.

"I don't know. How are you feeling?" I deflected, so we didn't talk about our impending fate.

"Do you think Storm will find us soon? I want to go home."

"Me too."

"They're looking for us, right?" Emilee tucked her knees into her chest, wrapping her arms around them, tiny trembles working through her body.

"Yes. The whole club is looking for us." I tried to not think negatively. Tried to not let my mind wander to a dark place. If Storm and his brothers hadn't rid the area of Hunters the last two months or found them, how would they find us now?

The dude returned with the water. Again, like the gum, he threw the bottles at us—jerk.

Emilee and I shared one bottle, saving the second. We chewed the gum with solemn expressions. Hero and Tara were awake, neither made a sound.

A chill crept up my spine as the prospect ogled me. I was only in my bra and panties. The asshole prez wouldn't give my clothes back. I'd never been assaulted and humiliated quite like this. Dane might have beat me when I let my mouth run, but every degrading word spewed, or the forced sex had been in private.

I choked down saliva, not allowing my mind to go to that dark, evil place. These men, the Hunters, were capable of far more heinous acts than hitting and making me strip. What they might do to the girls and I would change us in immeasurable ways. Death might be a better deal than the vile things they could do.

I needed to keep their focus off Emilee. She was so young.

God, I felt guilty and helpless.

Sometime later, the door swung open. Sunlight flooded the dimly lit room so bright I squinted, unable to make out who entered the silo. As my eyes adjusted after the door closed, I recognized the president. The enforcer followed with a crowbar in hand.

Lightheaded and nauseous, I pressed one hand to my stomach and grabbed Emilee's hand with the other as if she could protect me, sensing that vile man had come for me.

"Good afternoon. Lovely day isn't it?" The prez had an evil glint in his black eyes. "Hope you slept well. You'll need lots of energy to endure what I have in store for you." He locked his perverted gaze on me.

My blood turned cold as the prez made his way in my direction.

Emilee trembled against me. "Oh, God."

"Shhh." My heart hammered against my ribs. He wanted me. That much, I was sure.

"Look at you, *niñita*. I've been thinking of your tight cunt all night." He squatted, skimming his finger over my shoulder and down my arm. "If your man doesn't agree to my terms, I'll be having my way with you." He forcefully grabbed my face and tilted it up. He licked his lips. "That's right, *niñita*… That means little girl. I will own you, *niñita*."

"I'd rather die!" I couldn't stop myself from spitting in his face.

He wiped his cheek with the back of his hand. "You little cunt." He hissed through gritted teeth.

I saw his fist coming and braced for the impact, like I would do when Dane hit me. It didn't help. I was knocked back into the metal wall. Emilee cried out, so did I, seeing stars.

Hero growled and struggled in his chair, clanging it around as if it would help. It was no use. He was tied up and gagged, like Tara.

The prospect laughed at him.

Tears burned their way down my face as I touched my eye. I was bleeding. I'd never been punched like that before. Dane sprained my arm and bruised my body, shaking me when angry. He'd been careful with my injuries, so my friends wouldn't notice. Always knew where to hit that would be covered up by clothes. He'd kicked me in the stomach, but he never once punched me in the face.

The prez grabbed me by the arm, forcing me to my feet. "You're going to be fun to break, *niñita*. I will break you." He dragged me away from a sobbing Emilee. "How do you want her? Tied to the table?"

My heart felt like it jumped into my throat when I noticed the other man who'd entered the silo with the prez. I'd forgotten about him while the prez terrorized me.

Dane stalked toward me, his thumbs hooked in his pant's pocket, a smug expression. I was stunned silent. What was he doing with the Hunters?

"Hi, babe. Thought I told you to stay away from bikers?" Dane lifted my chin, taking in my appearance. "Fuck, you're a mess. Been running your mouth off, haven't you?

As it trembled, my lip betrayed me. My left eye was already swelling, hardly able to open it.

"I should've been firmer with you, so you'd obey better. I'm sorry about that." He stuck his thumb in my mouth, making me open it like before.

I could still read his mind. "No..." I cried, twisting my body, trying to break free of the prez's grasp. "Don't do this." Spit dribbled down my jaw as I gagged. "You'll never survive it. Storm will kill you." I slobbered, getting my words out.

Dane barked out a mocking laugh. "Babe, you're stupider than I thought. If Storm tries anything, he'll go to jail. I don't know what he wants with someone like you. You're much too vanilla."

Hero and Tara writhed in their chairs with a wild fury. Neither one could save me from whatever Dane and the prez would do.

I was on my own.

Dane removed his finger, trailing it down my throat. His eyes darted toward Emilee.

"Why are you here?" I shouted to get his attention back on me.

Dane smirked. "To sample the goods, of course. My friend and I have an arrangement." He glanced at Emilee again. I had to keep his focus on me or he'd do something rash to her.

"Dane!" My heart thumped hard in my chest. I knew that sick, lustful look in his eyes. Jesus, he wanted Emilee.

"If I keep the heat off him, I get my way with his product and some fun money. When he told me he had Storm's ol' lady, well, I had to see for myself." His finger moved to the cut on the corner of my eye. I winced as he dug his nail into it. "Shoulda kept your mouth shut, babe. I don't like seeing your pretty face busted up." He lowered his mouth to mine.

I turned away from him. "No!"

He gripped my face. "Don't be a bitch. You know saying *no* means nothing to me." He forcefully kissed me, but I kept my lips closed. He growled, "I want you on your fucking knees, bitch." He unhooked his belt, a revolting expression on his face.

The prez pushed me down. "You heard the deputy, *niñita*."

A sob rattled in my chest as I heard Emilee behind me. Hero

grunted and huffed, practically losing his mind.

Being forced by these monsters to suck Dane's dick wasn't the worst thing they could do to me. I had given him blow jobs before. I could block it out. If I was difficult, there could be blowback on the others… on Emilee.

Dane dropped his pants. "Open wide, babe."

"Not in front of the others. Please, Dane."

"I love it when you beg. But no dice." He dropped his boxers and palmed his unimpressive, pathetically small dick.

Bile shot into my throat. I gagged on stomach acid. Where was Storm? Why hadn't he found us yet?

"Still a drama queen." Dane slapped me. "Gag and throw up all you want. I won't mind."

I knew it wouldn't, because he was a sick fuck.

"If you fight or bite me, I'll have them strap you to the table, spread eagle. We'll all take a turn with you… and the girl." He jerked his head toward Emilee. "Understand?"

The prez yanked on my hair, lifting my face toward Dane. Having an audience was one thing. Doing this in front of my friends and Hero was different. Jesus, I'd never been so humiliated.

Hero grunted, trying to talk.

Tara and Emilee sobbed.

It was surreal. Like the worst nightmare I'd ever had.

"It's okay, Hero," I said in a calm voice. "Don't watch. Please, none of you watch." Tears streamed down my face. I felt so pathetic for crying, for letting them break me.

Wasn't this what I deserved after getting us in this position in the first place? If I had only listened to Storm, we wouldn't be here.

"Open wide," Dane hissed. "I'm tired of waiting. If you don't make it good for me, you'll be on the table. Ya hear?"

I'm dying inside. God, help me.

I closed my eyes and opened my mouth.

CHAPTER TWENTY-THREE

STORM

We were in position at Johnson's Organic Farm. Ready to storm the grounds and rescue Madeline and the others.

I drew my forty-five as we crept toward the silo. Beads of sweat dripped down my temples, hands slick and sticky as my heart raced with anticipation. I was so damn nervous.

Eighteen bikers surrounded the hobby farm, which had been part of a large-scale operation back in the day. Two silos separated the outbuildings and the corn crops. We were fortunate it wasn't something short like soybeans. The corn was tall enough to hide us as we moved through it.

We divided into three groups of six. Miguel and his men were with me, Boxer and Track coming from the south side. My dad and his crew took the east side with Lynx. The last group led by Raul, Justin, and Ire had the north side with brothers from my club.

This many men could have been overkill. The Knights had already taken out six Hunters, but we had no clue how many there were. Throw a dirty deputy into the mix; I wasn't sure what we were walking into.

All I knew was I couldn't take another second without my Angel. I was weak without her. Dead inside. Soulless.

If Deputy fuckin' Miller and any other law enforcement from Winters was here, Sheriff Hendrick's and his men would handle it. They were driving onto the farm.

"There." Boxer pointed as we looked through binoculars.

From my vantage point, I watched three Hunters run toward the silos. I couldn't tell which one they went to. Without wasting another second, I gave the command to move into my earpiece.

Boxer led our group, gun drawn. My heart pumped like an oil rig with such force I might explode. Everyone had orders to only shoot and kill if shot at first. I didn't want a bloodbath. But I also wasn't going to let these fuckers live.

We rounded the perimeter of the silo closest to us. I dialed in to what I thought was a woman sobbing. Silos were made of steel, so I wasn't sure if I'd imagined the cries.

"The three maggots entered the can closest to us," came Raul's voice in my earpiece.

"We got the other," I replied.

As we turned the corner, Boxer's hand went up, stopping us. He didn't hesitate to take out the Hunter. Even with a silencer on his gun, the whizzing sound was heard. The piece of shit made a loud grunt, hitting the dirt.

"What the fuck?" was shouted from inside the structure.

"Move," I hissed.

The metal door swung open as Deputy Miller rushed out, gun drawn. Boxer had the gun knocked out of Miller's hands and handcuffed him before the sonofabitch could react. The sight of his pants, opened at the fly, had me reeling. I'd deal with Miller later.

Miguel and I barreled into the silo with Track behind us. My eyes instantly landed on my Angel, on her knees in only a bra and panties. Our eyes connected and my heart died when I noticed the dirty fucker holding a gun to her head.

"There are only three," Track muttered from behind. "I've got the left."

"I have dead center," Miguel shouted, referring to the Hunter's prez, Dawg.

I flicked my eyes to the right where Emilee was sobbing.

"Found me did you, ese?" Dawg rasped. He used Madeline as a human shield.

"Let her go, Diego. I might let you live." Miguel slowly stepped forward. He wanted the prez, and I'd told him he could have him. Now I wished I hadn't. "Tell your men to stand down."

Dawg sneered. "Take them out. I don't give a fuck about them."

The guy I had my gun on whipped his head toward *Diego*.

"What the fuck, Prez?" the Hunter protested.

Yeah, his prez didn't acknowledge him. Nor did he give a shit about anyone else but himself. The boy was smart and laid his gun on the ground, kicking it toward me. He raised his hands in surrender. Good boy.

I pushed the piece behind me, keeping mine on him.

"You motherfucker," shouted the dude Track had his gun on. I believed he was the enforcer, the one who raped Ava. He wouldn't live to see his next birthday if I had anything to say about it.

"I'm not going down without a fight," the prez said. "Defend me."

"Fuck you, ese." The enforcer surrendered his weapon. I noticed Hero and Tara bound behind him. Fuck. Hero's face was hardly recognizable.

"I'll kill your ol' lady Storm," Deigo said in a lethal tone. "Let me go, and I'll let her live."

Madeline's baby-blues were on me, tears rolling down her

swollen, bruised face. I fuckin' wanted this to be over so I could take her into my arms and never let her go.

"You aren't leaving this can alive," Miguel gritted out. "My brother is on fucking life support. Take the bitch out. The second you do, you're next."

My heart seized. Why the fuck would Miguel tell this whack job to kill my woman? That wasn't part of the plan.

"Miguel," I whisper-shouted.

"I got this," he replied.

Diego pressed the gun into Madeline's temple. "It'd be a shame to rid the world of such a fine piece of pussy."

Motherfucker. It took every ounce of restraint to not lose my mind.

"I'm coming in loud," Boxer said. We were all wearing earpieces so Track and Miquel heard him too. My crazy-ass brother liked to get theatrical, create a diversion. It was our chance to take the motherfuckin' maggot down. "Three... two... one..."

"Angel, down!" I yelled as the door flew open. Boxer roared like a fuckin' madman.

I dove for my woman as shots flew above me, shielding her with my body. Miguel's gun went off. He didn't stop firing until he'd emptied his clip into Diego. The Hunter prez was gone, snuffed out like a candle.

The only door to the silo opened again. Several of my brothers ran in, Justin leading the pack.

"Daddy," Emilee cried, reaching her arms out.

Justin rushed toward her, wrapping her in his arms. "Emilee. Thank God."

I turned my attention back to my Angel. "Baby, did I hurt you?" I lifted off her small, nearly naked body, helping her up. "Are you hurt anywhere?" I softly touched the cut near her eye.

She shook her head, grabbing onto me as she sobbed. "No, I'm okay."

Goddamn, the bastard fucked up her face. I removed my black T-shirt and put it on her. "You're safe now, Angel. I'm so damn sorry this happened to you. So damn sorry," I said around the lump in my throat.

"Just hold me. Don't let go." She curled into my arms, burying her face in my neck. "Don't let go… don't let go."

"Never, Angel. Never letting you out of my sight again." Finally, I felt whole. Like I could breathe.

"Emilee!" Dodge ran toward her.

She pulled out of Justin's arms and fell into Dodge's. "Danny. Oh God, Danny."

"Did they hurt you, my sweet girl?" He took her face into his hands and kissed it all over.

"No, but I've never been so scared."

"I'll never let anything happen to you again. What about…" His voice trailed as his hand went to her stomach."

The look of utter shock on Justin's face was palpable. We hadn't told him about Emilee and Dodge. All hell was sure to break loose any second, but I had no intention of sticking around for it. I needed to get my woman home.

Hendricks put his hand on my shoulder. I hadn't even noticed him. "Is she okay?"

I stood, cradling her in my arms. "I'm not sure. I'm taking her back to the clubhouse so Patch can run a checkup. Miller was here."

Madeline trembled in my arms, still hiding her face in my neck. I squeezed her tighter to my body.

"Saw him." Hendricks shook his head. "Only one dead, good job. I'll take care of it. I'll need her statement." He looked at Madeline.

"Not now. Drop by the club later." I glanced at Hero and Tara. "I'm sure they can tell you everything that happened."

The sheriff patted my back. "I'm sure you're right."

"We can't leave Tara here," Madeline whispered. "Please, she has to come with me."

Track had just cut Hero loose and was doing the same for Tara.

I went over to him. "You bring them to the club. I don't want anyone other than Hendricks talking to Tara."

Track nodded. "Got it."

With that, I carried my woman out of the silo and into the sunshine.

My dad approached. "I got the truck right over here." He eyed Madeline. "Christ," he gritted out, his expression pained.

"We'll be in the truck. I want Hero and Tara riding with us. Track is with them inside," I told him as I walked away.

"I'll get them." He pushed the keys into my hand.

I got us situated in the backseat so Hero could sit in the front. I had no idea what his injuries were and didn't want him struggling to squeeze into the back. Madeline was in her spot on my lap. She hadn't lifted her head once, pressing her body into mine as if trying to hide inside me.

I held her tightly. Pouring my love into her.

My eyes landed on Deputy fuckin' Miller handcuffed, leaning against the sheriff's car. Blood boiled through every one of my veins.

"What's wrong?" she whispered, turning toward the window. Of course she would notice the change in me. Just as I felt her body stiffening when she saw Miller.

"Oh." She said nothing else, burying her face in my neck.

"It's okay, Angel. I'm here." I rubbed her back the way she liked. "I'm here."

Goddamn, I wanted to jump out of the truck and tear him to pieces with my bare hands.

Now wasn't the time for retribution. Once she was healed, I'd avenge my Angel so she never had to worry about seeing that prick again.

CHAPTER TWENTY-FOUR

MADELINE

We're safe was all I could think about since arriving at the club. Their prez was dead. I wasn't sure what would happen to the rest of his members. If they'd go to jail or if Storm and his brothers would take care of them. Their fate didn't really matter to me. I just wanted them gone.

I'd been in a dorm room holding Tara for the last half hour while Patch took care of Hero. His physical injuries were the worst of all of us. Of course I pissed off Storm when I didn't let Patch examine me first. And for not letting him in the room with Tara and me.

I got it. Storm had the life scared out of him and was worried about my well-being. I loved him for it. Adored his protectiveness. But Tara and Hero were my priority.

"I'm so sorry about this," I said softly for the fifth time. "I should've listened to Storm and stayed on the compound."

Tara shook her head. "Don't blame yourself, Mads. I know you'd never do anything to hurt me or the others. I saw what you did to protect Emilee." Her body trembled as fresh tears rolled down her face. "I hurt for all you've been through during this ordeal. Then that fucking Dane... What he..."

"Shh, I don't want to talk about it. I just want to be sure you're okay. What happened before they brought you to the silo?" I hadn't wanted to ask, fearing the worst. But I needed to know to help her the best I could.

"They had Hero and me in the other silo. He was unconscious. They said they were going to torture him if Storm wouldn't give up Winters for you." She sniffled, wiping her eyes with a tissue.

"Then what?"

A sob bubbled out of her. "He... he... tried to rape me."

"Oh, God." I tugged her into my arms. "Who?"

"The Latino."

She was talking about the enforcer—the same man who raped Ava.

"I fought him off, screaming and kicking. Another one tried to hold me down as the Latino punched me." She pulled back, staring me in the eyes. "Hero came to and knocked him off of me. Even with his hands tied behind his back, he fought them. I'm so glad those idiots hadn't tied up his feet."

"Jesus." My eyes dropped to her chest. "Is the blood on your shirt from the enforcer punching you?"

"No. Hero smashed his head into the young dude's mouth who was holding me down. He lost two teeth."

"Wow."

"Yeah. I've never seen a raging man before. Hero saved me."

"But you were gone a long time. You both looked bad off when they brought you in." There had to be more that happened.

"The prez and a couple more bikers stopped Hero's beatdown on the Latino." Tara paused to blow her nose. "They all took a turn beating him." Her lip trembled. "I thought they might kill him."

"Oh, sweetie." I hugged her. "I'm so sorry. If I could turn back time…"

"Stop it, Mads. I know what you're doing. What happened isn't your fault."

"Yes, it is." I choked up. "I don't know how to live with myself for causing everyone so much pain."

Tara gripped my shoulders. "Storm! Storm!"

"What are you doing?"

The door swung open and my man appeared. "What's wrong?"

"She needs you," Tara told him. "She's talking stupid. Blaming herself."

"Tara." I took her hand. "I'm not leaving you."

"Mads, I'm shaken up. My face hurts. But babe, I'll be okay. What you went through—"

"Stop." I glared into her eyes, pleading for her to not say another word. "I won't leave you."

"Sugar," Storm called out the door. "She'll stay with Tara. Patch is ready for you, baby."

I shook my head. "No. He needs to take care of Tara first."

"Jesus, Mads." She squeezed my hand. "Stop putting yourself last. You matter, too."

"Yes, she does." Storm squatted at my feet. The agony in his eyes gutted me. "Please, Angel. Let me take care of you."

"I'll stay with Tara as long as she needs me." Sugar put her hand on my shoulder. "Let Patch check you over."

I sighed, knowing I wouldn't win this battle. "Call me if you need anything." I hugged Tara. "Please. Anything."

"She's staying at the club until further notice, Angel. You can see her later," Storm said in a tone that left no room to argue.

"Really?" I reached for him, gratitude flooding my chest.

"Yeah, baby. Really. Come on. Patch is waiting." Storm tugged me into his arms and hoisted me up. He hadn't let me walk since the rescue.

"Storm?" Tara stood.

He stopped and turned us around.

She wrapped her arms around her middle. "How is he... Hero?"

"He's a mess but he'll be alright."

My heart died a little at how much fear was in her eyes.

"Can I see him?" Tara asked.

Storm nodded. "Maybe later. Patch gave him a sedative so he'd rest."

"Okay." Tara sat on the bed. Sugar closed the door behind us.

I laid my head on Storm's shoulder. "I'm sorry to be so much trouble."

"You're not any trouble, Angel. Just frustrating."

"I'm sorry." Tears pooled in my eyes.

"Stop with the 'I'm sorry.' You did nothing wrong. I should've got those bastards out of the area sooner."

"No, I—"

"Enough," he snapped. "Let's get you fixed up. We'll talk about all this later."

"Okay." It wasn't really okay, though. I didn't want to talk about anything that happened. I knew Storm would take full responsibility. It was just who he was, and it was admirable. But it was me who didn't listen to him—me who begged to take Emilee to the school.

I was drowning in guilt and regret.

Patch cleaned and sealed the cut near my eye with something he called liquid stitches. Tension rolled off Storm as he hung back, giving Patch space to do his job. Not for one second did I think Storm was angry with me. His fury was pointed at himself and the Dirty Hunters. And Dane. Still, I didn't like seeing him on the edge of detonation.

"Now that I've fixed your cuts, is there anything else I should know about?" Patch blocked my view of Storm. He was tall and lean, partially bald with white hair. "I can have him leave," he said in a low voice.

Storm didn't growl as I expected when Patch hid me. I understood Patch's meaning and shook my head. "No. Nothing else." Although I wondered if he had a pregnancy test. I was desperate for confirmation of my feelings. "But I do need something."

Patch eyed me with concern. "Storm, can you—"

"No, he can stay." I raised my voice in a panic. I didn't want Storm or Patch to get the wrong idea.

"Angel?" Storm stepped forward, a questioning glint in his stormy eyes.

"Dear, if you were assaulted, I can give you the morning-after pill. I'd want to examine you first, though." Patch's voice was hesitant as he held my gaze.

I reached my hand out to Storm. "No, I just wondered if you had a pregnancy test. My period is over a week late."

Patch's features softened. "Yes, I'll grab one." He went to his bag on the dresser.

Storm stared at me with no emotion on his face. I wasn't sure why he would be upset. He'd wanted a baby longer than me. Finding out I was pregnant might bring a little light into the darkness, following Storm and me. His face didn't show any sign of what I expected.

"Hey, what's wrong?" I pulled his hand toward me.

He sat and cradled my cheek softly. "It's just. What those animals did to you." He kissed my forehead. "Your stomach. Is it okay? They didn't hit you there, did they?"

Now I understood what was going on. He was smoldering inside. The tiniest spark would ignite a deadly fire. I needed to get him alone to soothe him. "No, they didn't."

"Here you go, Madeline." Patch handed the box to me. "Do you want to take it now?"

"I'll do it in our bedroom. Thank you, Patch." I smiled softly.

There was a knock at the door. "Storm?"

"It's Justin." Storm stood and released my hand. He opened the door, keeping me hidden. "Everything okay?"

"I need to talk to you," Justin said in a distressed tone.

"I'm busy."

"It won't take long. Please. It's about Emilee and me."

I understood Justin's fierce protectiveness for his daughter, but I couldn't help but worry about Emilee. Justin had locked her away the moment we arrived on the compound. I was sure she wanted to be with Dodge after the hell she'd been through.

Justin didn't seem to care. He didn't even want Patch touching her. I'd assured Storm and Patch, Emilee hadn't been touched, but a therapist might be a good idea. For all of us, really, after going through hell. The fear and uncertainty we experienced would mess up anyone. We might have come out mostly intact physically, but that shit left scars on our brains, on our souls. My wounds would heal in a couple of weeks. But the events of the last twenty-fours would remain inside me forever.

"I'm with Madeline," Storm hissed.

"I know. And I'm sorry. But I want out," Justin whispered. Patch and I looked at each other.

"Shit. Gimme fifteen minutes. I'll meet you in my office. Find Raul." Storm shut the door without waiting for a reply from Justin.

"I'll be okay," I assured him as I stood.

He reeled me into his arms. "This is bullshit. I need to be with you, Angel. I don't want you alone."

"Tina or Sugar can stay with me. I'll just take a shower. Get the grime off me. I'm disgusting."

"I should be the one helping you with that." He pressed his lips to my temple. His heart thumped rapidly against my chest. Was he angry with Justin? Or afraid to let me go?

"I know, baby. And you will."

Be strong for him. Don't let him break.

CHAPTER TWENTY-FIVE

STORM

I'd called Tina to stay with Madeline once we got to our bedroom. I didn't want to leave my Angel. Not for a second. It was hard enough waiting in the hallway when she was in Tara's room. The distance away from Madeline killed me, but I'd relented for her.

Now I hugged her, trying to rip myself away to go downstairs to deal with Justin. I wasn't strong enough for this shit. I needed a break. Needed my woman in my arms and the rest of the fuckin' world to stay out of our way.

She kissed my neck. "I'll be okay." The sound of her voice didn't match her words. She was putting up a good front, but I knew better. Like me, she was barely holding on.

I dug my phone out of my pocket. "I'll call Raul. He can deal with Justin."

She covered my hand with hers. "No, I'm okay."

"You're not, Madeline. After everything you just went through. You can't hide it from me. You're slowly crumbling. I need to be here for you like you've always been for me." I softly brushed my thumb along her jaw.

Was she out of her ever-loving mind? Maybe she was after the nightmare she'd gone through.

"Please. It sounds serious. I heard Justin say he wanted out. Out of the club, right?"

Tina gasped. "Sorry." She grimaced.

"See? This is serious, Storm. Go handle it. I'll be here. Tina's with me."

I cradled her face in my hands, careful to not hurt her. "Fine. Call me if you need me. I'll come running. I won't be long."

"I'm just going to clean up." Her face twisted in disgust.

"I'll be back before you're finished." I dropped a kiss on the tip of her nose to avoid her bruised cheeks.

"I'm sure you will." Her voice sounded strong. Damn, she was convincing. But she didn't fool me. The faster I went to settle this shit with Justin, the faster I could return to her. Then nobody better bother us until I gave the all-clear.

"Tina, if she needs anything," I told her in a warning tone, "call me."

"I have my phone right here." She shook it in front of her.

"I hate leaving you after I just got you back, Angel."

Her hand cradled my cheek. "Then hurry back to me." She pushed me toward the door. "Go."

Reluctantly, I left my whole world again. I stalked down the stairs, pissed as fuck. The rumble of voices eddied out of the bar. My dad's louder than the rest. I turned the corner, heading down the hallway toward my office. When I entered, Justin and Raul were waiting for me.

"Let's get this done. My woman needs me," I barked out, shutting the door, not caring about anyone else's feelings. I dropped into my chair and leveled my eyes on Justin.

"I want out—today. I'm taking my Emilee and leaving." Justin held an unyielding gaze.

I dragged my hand down my face. Tired. I was so fuckin' exhausted. "I get it, brother. The last couple of days have been hell. I want to take Madeline away and hide from the rest of the world, but I can't. The club is our life."

Justin shook his head. "No. Emilee is my life. I almost lost her. Laura must've been turning in her grave." He teared up, shaking his head. "I'm out. For my daughter's safety, I gotta go."

Raul looked sidelong at Justin. "Emilee's an adult, Justin. She's in love with my nephew. They're having a baby."

Justin flew out of his chair, pointing his finger at Raul. "I don't give a fuck about your nephew! Every man in the club knows to stay away from my daughter. My. Daughter. I should beat him within an inch of his life." He gripped his head between his hands. "She's all I have. She'll go where I say she goes!"

Dammit, I knew where Justin was coming from. If it were me in his shoes, I'd drag my kid kicking and screaming too.

"So you just want out?" I asked. "Why not take a leave of absence. A couple of weeks or a month. Clear your head, but don't quit the club. Don't turn in your cut."

"My mind is made up. Put it to a vote." Justin exhaled a labored breath. "Now, preferably. I have Emilee packing. I want to go as soon as possible."

I flicked my eyes to Raul. "Do we have enough members in the bar to vote?"

Raul sighed, lifting out of the chair. "Yeah. I'll get Hero's proxy and explain what's going on to the rest in the bar." He left the office.

I leveled my gaze at Justin as I rocked in my chair. "A leave of absence would be better. If I fill your spot at the table, that's it. You can't get it back."

"I know, Storm. I'm not going to change my mind. I'm too old for the club life. Too damn tired to be a one-percenter. Living and dying for the club isn't what I want anymore. I need to think about Emilee."

"Does she know you're getting out?"

His eyes went to the floor as he leaned against the wall, shoving his hands into his pockets. "No. I'm taking her back to school and will stay with her. Find an apartment where she can live with me. I'll get a job. Have a normal life."

I snorted. "There's no such thing as normal, brother. You know that."

"I need to do this, Storm. I won't put her life in danger again."

Justin wasn't a fool. He was unhinged. Having the shit scared out of a person did that. If he wanted out of the club, I'd let him go.

"You could talk to Abe. See if he knows of any job prospects." Fargo wasn't far from my cousin's territory. He'd know what's available.

"Nah. I want no affiliation to the Knights. Sorry, brother."

I stood and went to the door. "Let's get this over with so I can get back to my woman."

Everyone was gathered in the bar. I could cut the tension with a knife, it was so thick. Not once had a member wanted out. Only two members had ever been kicked out of the club, years before my time as president.

"Brothers," I shouted. "Do you understand what this vote is for?"

They grunted.

"Justin wants out of Knight's Legion MC. His position at the table as secretary will be open. A new member will be voted in by the council when I deem the time is right. Understand?"

They grunted.

I put my arm on Justin's back. "Are you sure?"

He issued a short nod. "Yes."

In a situation like this, it wasn't likely anyone would vote against Justin leaving the club. A vote was a futile part of the process. So rather than ask who was in favor, I asked, "Does anyone oppose releasing Justin from the club?" I scanned the bar, making eye contact with my brothers. Not one spoke.

"Where is she?" Dodge stormed into the bar. So much for no one speaking. Heads turned his way.

"None of your goddamn business," Justin yelled. "Stay away from my daughter or I'll kill you."

Shit, I didn't need this. "Track. Boxer." I jerked my head toward Dodge. They both grabbed an arm and held him back. It did no good. Dodge was a big motherfucker. I understood his desperation, but he'd betrayed Justin's trust. It was time for him to learn a hard, painful lesson.

Justin pointed his finger at him. "If you go near my daughter, you're dead."

"She's my woman. I claimed her. You can't keep her from me." Dodge struggled to get loose from Track and Boxer. "She's having my baby, you sonofabitch," he roared, getting red in the face.

My phone stole my attention in my back pocket. I took it out and my heart jolted. "Tina, what is it?"

"You need to get up here now," she choked out through tears.

"Raul put him in the quiet room. Handle the rest," I shouted, running out of the bar.

My bedroom door was open, Tina waited beside it. "She went in to shower and has been sobbing. The door is locked. I couldn't get in. I'm sorry."

I checked the doorknob like an idiot. "Angel, open the door." Jesus, I was fuckin' stupid. Like she could hear me over the shower and her wailing.

My heart thundered in my chest as I heard my woman in agony. The door locked from the inside and didn't have a key so I kicked the door open. Dramatic? I didn't fuckin' care. I was desperate to get to my girl. Tina and I rushed in.

I choked back a gasp, seeing Madeline on the shower floor, curled into a ball.

"Fuck, baby." I pulled off my boots and cut. "I got this, Tina." I ripped off my T-shirt and unzipped my jeans. "Lock the bedroom door on your way out."

She was gone as my jeans came off.

Stepping into the shower, I scooped up my girl and sat with her on the floor. "Baby, I'm here. I've got you."

Her arms went around my waist, clinging to me as her sobs filled the steamy air in the shower. Jesus, I died inside. I should've never left her. I knew she was hanging on by a thread, and I let her down *again*.

"It's my fault. I should've listened to you. I'm so so sorry."

I held the back of her head with one hand, the other wrapped around her. It wasn't enough to stop her body from shaking. She was so undone I doubted she'd hear anything I said. I knew the state she was in. The personal hell where she'd locked herself. I knew that place intimately, having lived in it for twelve years after Tommy's death.

But my Angel? The light in my darkness? She should never be in such a desolate place. I wouldn't let her drown in guilt like I had all those years, filled with anger and hatred toward myself.

No, I wouldn't let my beautiful, kind, loving woman fall. I wouldn't let her break. Or shut down. I'd carry her, pour my strength into her.

It wasn't time for words—only tenderness, understanding, and love.

I reached for her shampoo, lathering up her wet hair. I messaged her scalp, hoping it would relax her. By the time I conditioned her hair and rinsed the suds out, she'd calmed a little. Helping her to her feet, I braced her against my chest. I squeezed her favorite body wash onto a poof and cleaned her backside. Madeline rested her head on my chest, her body still trembling as she exhaled several times. I felt her release some tension. She let me pull her away to wash her front, arms, and legs. I went slow, hoping to relax her further.

My chest burned, feeling like it would cave in. I hurt so goddamn much for my Angel. What happened with the Hunters wasn't her fault. She and her friends should've been able to go out without fear of being taken. Nobody should be afraid to go outside their home. To go to the store or out to lunch. But evil had roamed the earth since the beginning of time. Being my woman put a target on her back, bringing danger straight for her.

Hell, as much as I wanted to take the blame, I had to accept it wasn't all my fault. The Dirty Hunters were vile and corrupt. A group of lowlifes. They didn't care about anything or anyone but themselves. Dawg was a selfish monster. My club did everything we could to drive them out of Minnesota. But they'd had Deputy Fuckin' Miller's help. No wonder we couldn't find where they'd been hiding. Miller would get his. He'd rue the day he ever messed with my woman.

I turned the water off once Madeline's body was free of soap. After squeezing the water out of her hair, I opened the glass door and reached for a large towel. She walked into it as I held it open. I dried her off, then myself.

"Come on, baby." I picked her up, cradling her in my arms, and carried her to bed.

CHAPTER TWENTY-SIX

MADELINE

Hours after being rescued, I was curled into a tight ball in bed with Storm's massive body wrapped around mine. The warmth radiating off him soothed me from the outside in. He kissed my head, whispering he loved me over and over. He made me feel cherished as he cared for my every need. I felt whole despite the hell I'd been through.

Storm was all I needed, a balm to my fractured spirit with a healing power like no other.

After he left to talk with Justin, I could hardly breathe. I didn't want to be a baby. Weak and pathetic needing my man when he had club business to attend to. I'd already caused enough chaos and pain to so many. So I pulled up my big girl panties and assured him I was okay. Naturally, it was a lie.

Not wanting to get into it with Tina, not that I thought she'd press me to talk, I had told her I was going to take a shower. She'd smiled sweetly, and in her quiet, comforting voice, told me she'd be right here if I needed anything. I knew she'd stay until Storm returned. I knew I could share with her the turmoil I was in. She'd understand. Wouldn't judge me. But the words never came.

In the bathroom, I'd stared at my battered body in the mirror. It was the first time I'd seen myself. God, I looked hideous. My face was swollen and red in some spots: black and blue in others. Dirt and dried on perspiration covered my body. I smelled like the silo. I'd flashed back to when Dawg forced me to strip. My stomach roiled, my heart racing as if his putrid breath was in the bathroom surrounding me. I felt his sticky hands on my breasts, grabbing my pussy. Then the memory of Storm watching that vile man assault me sent me over the edge... I lost it. Completely lost it.

I ran into the shower, even though it was too hot. I wanted to burn Dawg's touch off my skin, wipe him out of my memory. It didn't matter how hard I scrubbed. He wouldn't leave.

I'd screamed for Dawg to get out. Get out of my head. My home. My life. Falling to my knees, darkness engulfed me as I gasped for air in the suffocating steamy shower. Evil and guilt won, bending me to its will.

Now that I was calm in Storm's arms, I was sure Tina had banged on the bathroom door. I just hadn't heard her. Nor had I noticed Storm bursting through the door. Or anything he'd said to me.

But I'd felt his tender touch when he lifted me into his arms. Immersing me in his strength as I clung to him for dear life. He was my anchor. My protector. My everything.

After he washed and dried me, he didn't bother with clothes. We never slept in any, needing to be skin to skin. God, he knew exactly what I needed. Not once had he questioned what happened. He didn't ask if I was okay or what I needed. He just acted as if he heard my silent wishes.

Still, I sensed his fears and unrest as if it was my own. I imagined his mind raced with horrific thoughts of rape and torture. I heard his soul wailing in despair for not keeping me and the others safe.

I blew out a ragged breath, steeling myself. It was time I set his mind at ease. A little, anyway. I couldn't bring back AJ. Or magically erase Hero's injuries and the terror we all had endured. All I could do was put Storm's mind at rest.

I shifted in bed, rolling toward him, and wrapped my arm around his waist, nuzzling my face in his firm chest. I pecked soft kisses, inhaling him into my lungs. He rubbed soothing circles on my back, holding me close. No words. Just an enormous amount of love.

"I'm okay, Kaleb. Physically, I mean." Emotionally, it would take some time to heal.

His hand stopped moving as if hanging on my every word.

"They only hit me. Groped me some." I swallowed the emotion bubbling in my throat. I breathed him in, trying to draw his strength into me.

"You don't have to do this now, Angel." His lips dropped to my head, his hand moving again. "It's too soon. I just got you back."

"I do have to do this now. You need to know I wasn't assaulted… sexually." I peered up to his handsome face with my good eye, finding it strained.

"You can tell me, baby." His Adam's apple bobbed in his throat as he held me closer. Tension rolled off him in massive waves, threatening to pull me in under. I had to find a way to stay afloat. Stay strong for him. "If you want. I'm here for you."

I reached up, taking his face in my hands. "Look at me."

His stormy-gray eyes met mine. So much was going on behind them: anger, pain, guilt. I could see it so well he didn't have to tell me. He didn't need to feel responsible. I was to blame, me and only me.

"I wasn't raped. I swear I wasn't." I paused as my mind wandered to Tara. I'd feared the worst for her, but Hero had saved her. I was so grateful for his valor. Except they beat him for it. I shook myself out of my thoughts before they took me back into the hole Storm had dug me out of not long ago.

Storm carefully observed me. The corner of his lip twitched. Doubt crossed his beautiful face. Did he not believe me?

I rubbed the palm of my hand over his beard. "Did you hear me? I wasn't sexually assaulted."

"When we arrived, moments before barrelling into the silo, Miller stumbled out with his jeans hanging off his hips. You were on your knees." A shuddered breath vibrated in his chest, rattling mine.

I gripped his face firmly. "No. Do you hear me? Whatever you're thinking, stop. Dane wanted me to... blow him. But we heard one of the prospects scream. Dane had just entered my mouth but pulled out before anything happened."

"Fuck," Storm hissed, pulling out my hands. I caught a glimpse of tears before he hid his face in my neck. He squeezed the air out of me as he gasped. "I'm so sorry, Angel. I'm so goddamned sorry."

"It's not your fault. You saved me. Saved all of us. My badass biker boyfriend is my hero."

He growled against my skin. "But Miller—"

"But he didn't, Kaleb. He didn't. Yes, I was scared out of my mind. They threatened to rape Emilee and me if I didn't do as they said. I would do anything to protect her. Giving Dane a blow job wasn't the worst thing that could happen to me."

"Jesus..." A choked gasp ripped from his lungs. He shook his head as he kissed my shoulder, his tears leaving a trail behind his soft lips.

"I haven't been violated, baby." I rubbed the back of his head, down to his nape the way he liked. All I wanted was to soothe him as he'd done for me. Storm was strong and powerful but he felt pain deeply.

"Yes, you have. The way that motherfucker treated you on the camera. Forcing you to strip. Touching you. Goddammit, if Miguel hadn't killed him, I would've made that piece of shit wish he'd never been born." He reared his head back, a murderous glint in his watery eyes. But as soon as he met mine, they softened. The adoration in them speared into my heart, filling every empty nook.

"I wouldn't have stopped you," I told him honestly. "Men like Dane and the Dirty Hunters shouldn't walk freely. They should be locked in a cell or in hell."

Storm pressed his forehead to mine. "You're the most precious thing in my life. My Angel. My clear blue skies and sunshine. My heart. You chase away the darkness with your infectious radiance." He paused for a long second. "I let you down. I'll spend the rest of my life making it up to you. Protecting you with everything I am." He pulled back, staring into my eyes.

"Kaleb—"

His finger went on my lips. "I can't promise nothing like this will ever happen again. You know the life I live. The dangers being in the club brings. Yes, I blame myself for failing you. For failing so many. But you've taught me to let that shit go. I wasn't the only person involved in this. The Hunters are to blame for being vile bastards. Dawg got what was coming to him. The same for the others." His stormy eyes teared up again. "Just don't leave me. Don't walk away. Please?"

My vision blurred as he gazed at me like I was the most beautiful woman in the world. It was far from the truth with the bruises on my face. My left eye was swollen and half-open. Lip busted up. *You'd never know how horrific I was by the way he admired me.* But still…

"Don't say stupid shit, Kaleb. I'm not going anywhere. You're stuck with me. Until we're old and gray, rocking on the front porch, with our great-grandchildren fawning over your ancient Harley as if it were a national monument in a museum."

"I like the sound of that." He smiled, showing his perfectly white teeth. "I guess I need to build you a front porch."

I giggled. "I guess you do." Before I got swept away by the

beautiful image of my future with Storm, AJ entered my mind. "Kaleb?"

"Mhm."

"What about A…" His name caught in my throat, making me pause for a moment. "What about AJ? Will there be a funeral?" My body trembled as I remembered him getting shot.

He died because of me.

"Let's not do this now."

"Has anyone contacted his parents?"

The day Tommy died, the sheriff came to our home. Toby was with him. My mom broke down on the spot; dad stayed strong, eyes vacant. A piece of us died that day with Tommy. I was sure AJ's family would, too… because of me.

"Baby, AJ was estranged from his family. He never knew his dad. His mom was an addict with an abusive boyfriend who used AJ as a punching bag. Knight's Legion MC was the only family he cared about."

"Oh, God." I cried into Storm's chest. AJ had been through hell. Now he was gone. "We have to do something for him."

"We will, Angel. The club will have a service for him at the pond behind the club. It's where we release the ashes of the fallen."

I nodded, melting into his arms. "I want to see Emilee. Make sure she's okay."

Storm sighed, brushing his warm hand up and down my spine. "I'm sorry, but Justin isn't in a good place. He's taking her away from the club today. He might even be gone already."

I lifted my head, mouth gaping. "Really? I haven't even apologized to him for all of this. I need to see both of them."

"No you don't. Justin knows the nature of the club. The dangers it brings to those in it. He's grateful for all you did to protect Emilee."

I shook my head, staring into Storm's calm gray eyes, then dropped my face into his chest. What else was there to say? I had a massive crater in my heart with AJ, Emilee, Hero, and Tara's name on it. I didn't think I'd ever get past it or forgive myself.

"You're not to blame, Angel. Locking you up on the compound is no way to live. You should be free to go out to lunch and shop with your friends. It's my job to keep you and my territory safe. If anyone is to blame, it's me. Me alone."

I couldn't let him take full responsibility. He was right, though. My friends and I should've been able to go out for an afternoon. I shouldn't need a bodyguard. AJ shouldn't have been gunned down.

"I don't blame you," I whispered with my lips against his chest.

"And I don't blame you, baby. Not for a second. The Dirty Hunters are responsible. Let's direct our anger at them. Not ourselves." The strength in his voice seeped into my veins, blasting into my soul. Its healing powers released me from the unbearable grief eating my insides. I doubted I would ever fully forgive myself, but Storm was right. The Hunters were to blame. Not Storm. Not me.

Rolling onto my back, I pulled him onto my body. "Make love to me."

His eyebrows raised in surprise. "But it's only been a few hours since… You've just been through hell."

"You're right. I have. So shouldn't I get anything I want?"

He seemed to war with his choices, but his cock knew precisely what to do as it hardened against my pelvis.

I cradled his handsome face in my hands. "I want it nice and slow. Sweet and gentle. Can you do that for me?" I needed him more than ever before, desperate for his touch to wipe away the memory of Dane and Dawg putting their hands on me.

He dropped his lips to mine, carefully avoiding the busted corner. "Anything you want, Angel. You can stop me at any time." He kissed down the bend of my neck as he wedged himself between my legs.

This man. Always considerate of my well-being.

"I'll never stop you from loving me, Kaleb. Never." I hooked a leg around the back of his thigh, opening myself to him.

He put his hand between us, brushing a finger across my entrance. I wasn't dripping wet like usual, but I was getting there. I wasn't forcing sex. I needed the connection with our bodies as one the way they were meant to be.

"You're sure?" The worry in his eyes and the hesitancy in his voice made me feel cherished and loved. He'd rather die a million deaths than ever hurt me.

How did I ever get so lucky?

I took his cock in my hand and stroked him. "I'm sure, baby. Then we can sleep. I'm exhausted."

"So am I. I can't sleep when you're gone." He eased his way into me, gritting his teeth. "You're so tight."

I wasn't fully aroused, but I didn't care. I needed this. Needed him.

Exhaling, I relished feeling him fill every inch of me. "Yes... This is what I want."

He pulled out slowly, then slid back in. "When did you want to take the test?"

I gripped his biceps, a soft gasp leaving my lips with each one of his intentional thrusts. He never quite grasped the effect he had on me. How I couldn't speak when we made love.

"Angel?"

"Don't... need to." I panted, closing my eyes.

"Gimme your baby blues." A cocky smirk played on his handsome face. "Is my cock so fucking fantastic you can't speak?"

Damn him. He knew he stole my breath away. But I knew he was trying to keep my mind off all the awful shit. I adored him with every cell in my body.

"In my heart, I know I'm pregnant."

He kissed the tip of my nose. "Me too, Angel."

"Really? How?"

"I've noticed the changes in your body. You gave up coffee and took naps." His languid movements lulled me so perfectly. God, we were incredible together.

We're a fierce, impenetrable force.

I relished in the quiet of Storm's love, coming again and again against him.

CHAPTER TWENTY-SEVEN

STORM

It'd been a couple of weeks since the hell we'd all endured. Madeline was recovered physically, sans the small cut near her eye. Emotionally it would take some more time.

Today was AJ's memorial out at Wennberg Pond. I held Madeline close as we watched Raul release AJ's ashes. All club members, prospects, and kittens were in attendance.

There were also a few unexpected guests: Madeline's parents and my dad and his family. Too busy with my role in the memorial, I had yet to speak to any of them.

When the service was over, we congregated to the clubhouse for the barbecue.

My Angel was doing better. She was the fiercest woman I knew, but she wasn't indestructible. Or made of iron.

At the silo, she'd done what was needed for everyone's safety. Her sacrifice had left her emotionally fragile. She cried at the drop of a hat. Had nightmares every night. It cut me deep when I held her trembling body and listened to her whimpers until she settled back asleep. She tried like hell to resume her usual activities, like cooking with Sugar and Tina and hanging out in the bar with me. None of it was easy, yet she persevered—determined to not let the Hunters break her.

None of it had been easy for me either. The few times I needed to go into town to meet with Sheriff Hendricks tore me apart. I worried nonstop about Madeline, unable to relax until I had her in my arms.

Without asking, I led my girl to her parents' table. They'd wanted to come out to see us both after Madeline had called them last week. It just happened they could only come this weekend. Tara and Stephanie were seated at their table. Madeline's friends had been spending more time at the clubhouse. Tara had a room in the basement. Madeline had begged her to stay, not wanting her alone. Hero had demanded *Roja* remain at the compound. Between the two of them, of course I made Tara a home within our care.

"Mom, Dad." Madeline rushed over to them. She hugged one and then the other. Love filled the air. It wrapped around me like a vice, stealing the air from my lungs.

My chest tightened as I felt a familiar emotion: unconditional love. Neither shot me a glaring look. They were the same, kind folks I remembered.

"How are you, sweetie?" Mrs. Hamilton asked.

"Better." Madeline reached her hand out to me. "Remember Kaleb?" she whispered my name. "Call him Storm from now on."

"They don't have to, Angel." I nodded to Mr. and Mrs. Hamilton. "Sir." I extended my hand.

Thomas gave me a once-over before shaking. "I hardly recognize you, son."

My heart slammed into my chest. *Son.* It was what he used to call me.

Madeline squeezed my hand, tugging me out of my shock.

"Yes, sir. I've changed quite a bit. Mrs. Hamilton, it's good to see you." I'd never been so nervous. Did they blame me for what happened to Madeline? I'd been too chicken shit to ask if she'd told them about the Dirty Hunters—at least the parts I'd given her permission to talk about.

"Aww, it's Sara." She hugged me. "I'm sorry for your loss."

"Thank you. AJ was a good guy." We pulled back at the same time.

The four of us looked at each other, waiting for someone to speak. My heart raced as my imagination threatened to take me down a dark tunnel, to a life where I didn't have my Angel.

What if they convinced her to dump me?

"You can relax, son. We're not going to give you the third degree about anything. Maddy told us about the baby and how much she loves you. Congratulations, Daddy." Thomas winked, putting his hand on my shoulder. His easy-going attitude hadn't changed. I respected the hell out of him.

Daddy.

Shit, I needed a drink. In my pocket was the ring I'd bought Madeline weeks ago. When she told me her parents were coming to AJ's service, I figured it was the perfect time to ask for her dad's blessing. Thought he might want to see the ring.

Tonight, I planned to propose. No fancy dinner or anything, just me keeping it simple. I knew Madeline didn't want anything else. She'd said as much, a dozen times. Clearly, she suspected I'd ask her to marry me.

"We can't wait to be grandparents." Sara reeled Madeline in for a hug. "How've you been feeling, honey?"

"Let's sit." Madeline pulled out a chair.

"I'll get us some drinks." I needed a minute to regroup. The Hamiltons hadn't changed one bit. I hadn't needed to worry.

"I'll join you," Thomas said as I turned toward the bar.

"Copper, Jack and an IPA, lemonade for Angel. What will you have?" I asked Thomas.

"I like how you call her Angel." He studied me for a painfully long second. "Ask me." He smirked, then told Copper, "Two drafts."

Did he mean what I thought he meant? "Ask what, sir?"

"For my blessing." Always a straight shooter, like Madeline.

Copper set the whiskey in front of me. I tossed back my liquid courage and embraced the burn. "You know, I never imagined I'd fall in love and want to get married. Madeline changed all of that."

The pride and love in his blue eyes hit me square in the chest. "She's a remarkable woman."

"She is." I took a long pull of my beer. "I can't live without her."

"She told us the same about you. With a baby on the way, you'll be forever bound to each other. You ready for forever with Maddy?" He watched me earnestly.

"Yes." There was no question in my mind.

"No hesitation. That's all I needed. You have my blessing, son." He gave me a fatherly hug as Madeline made her way toward us.

She sidled up next to me. "Everything okay?"

"Just catching up, Angel." I dropped a kiss on her lips. Relief rushed through my veins now that I knew where I stood with Thomas.

My dad appeared. "Storm, Jane and I would like to meet your Angel."

"I'll take this to Sara." Thomas took the mugs of beer and left.

My dad hadn't met Madeline after the rescue. She'd hid in our bedroom for days. When he left, he said he'd be back soon. For once, he kept his word.

I put my arm around my girl and introduced her. "Angel, this is my dad, David and his wife, Jane."

"It's nice to meet you both." She shook their hands.

"The pleasure is ours." Jane waved over the girls. "These are our daughters, Hannah and Megan."

"Hi," Maddy waved.

My half-sisters sure had grown since the last time I saw them. Dad had told me they were in high school. Hannah was a junior and Megan was a freshman. I nodded to them.

It was strange watching my dad act like a family man. He was never this way with my mom. I wasn't sure how I felt about it.

"I want you to know, I'm happy Storm found you," my dad said. "I remember how he doted on you back home in Garrison. He called you a little firecracker. Of course, back then, you were a scrawny little girl. But you've blossomed into a beautiful woman."

Who the hell was this guy? I couldn't believe he remembered any of that. Jesus, I needed another shot.

Madeline giggled. "Thank you. We've both changed a lot. Has he told you the news?" She peered up at me.

I shook my head.

David narrowed his gaze. "What news?"

"Tell him." She patted my stomach.

"We're having a baby," I blurted like an idiot. Being around my dad made me fuckin' uncomfortable.

David's eyes bulged. "No shit? I'm going to be a granddad?" He grinned, his stormy gray eyes glittering. "Did you hear that, honey? We're going to be grandparents." He threw his arms around Madeline and me, hugging both of us at the same time.

Was I in the *Twilight Zone?*

"Thank you, Mr. Knight." Madeline fisted my shirt. I could read her like a book. She was just as confused and overwhelmed by my dad.

"David, call me David." He tightened his embrace and shook us. Excitement radiated off him. I swear, I'd never seen him this way before.

"When is the baby due?" Jane pulled David away and hugged us. All this acting like we were close was irritating me. But I held it together for my woman. She was having a good day despite her sadness over AJ. Talking about the baby always made her happy. I would endure anything to keep a smile on her pretty face.

"The end of May. I'm hoping our little peanut stays in until school is out." Madeline patted her belly and flicked her baby blues up to mine. Her returning to work was a sore subject. After everything she'd been through, she still wanted to start work the day after Labor Day. The only reason I agreed was that she promised to not leave the building. I'd drop her off and pick her up, and a prospect would sit in the parking lot all day.

"How wonderful! Are your parents excited? I bet they are. I'm hoping you'll bring the baby to Garrison often. Oh, it would be so wonderful to spend holidays together…" Jane ran away at the mouth. It wasn't fair to her, but I could hardly stomach being around the woman. I wasn't quite sure why. She seemed to make my dad happy and wasn't the reason my mom left. I'd just never met anyone, so… sugary sweet.

Movement out of the corner of my eye drew my attention. Hero stumbled in, a bottle of tequila in his hand. Dammit. I'd wondered where he went after the service.

"Excuse me." I interrupted Jane. She hadn't stopped talking. Not that I was listening to anything she said. I'd tuned her out. My dad had wandered off to Raul's table.

"I'll be back, baby." I kissed Madeline.

She peered around me toward Hero. "Sure. I hope he's okay. I'll be at my parents' table."

I went over to Hero and Track. "Hey, brother. Have you eaten?" I gripped Hero's bicep.

"Don't need food. I just wanted another bottle to take up to my room." Cheap tequila wasn't what he needed. The guy would be hugging the porcelain before the night was over.

I cut my gaze to Track's, then told Hero, "Let's get you some food first." My brother had been a mess, drinking himself into the gutter all week. He felt responsible for the Hunters getting the jump on him. He'd been in the silo when Dawg had hit Madeline and forced her to strip. Yeah, Hero was fucked up. Fighting demons of the past and what he viewed as another failure for not protecting AJ and the women.

I knew this kind of pain and was sure AJ's memorial didn't help. Hero wasn't handling the loss at all, hunkered down in his bedroom. I had to pull rank as his president and order him to stay in the clubhouse when he tried to leave. Patch wanted him watched, worried Hero was a danger to himself. Mentally, my brother was unstable. Survivor's guilt had him on edge. I wasn't sure what he might do. We were set to leave on the run Monday. I wanted him clear-headed.

"We need to get him sober," Track muttered, helping to hold up Hero.

Wobbling against us, Hero was hellbent on drowning himself in booze. I didn't want to put him in the quiet room, but if he didn't get his head straight in the next twenty-four hours, I'd have no other choice. His well-being was my priority.

Tara appeared beside us. "Storm, can I help? Please, I need to help him." The redhead's eyes were glossy.

Track and I stared at each other. She'd been begging to see Hero since the day they were rescued, but Hero had refused. He didn't want her anywhere near him. I didn't understand it.

Who was I to decide for him?

"You can ask," I told her, jerking my chin to Hero. Maybe Tara was what Hero needed like I had needed my Angel. My girl quieted my demons and healed me in ways I could never repay.

Tara went in front of him. "Hey, big guy. Let's blow this joint and find a quiet place."

Hero raised his head. "Rooojjjaaa." He swayed on his feet. "Fuuuck." His head bobbled as he checked her out. The dude was so wasted he didn't even finish talking and closed his eyes.

She reached up and took his face in her hands. "Look at me." He peeled his eyes open. "Let's get out of here, okay?"

"Not off the compound," I whispered, even though I was sure she knew better, but I wouldn't take any chances with my SAA. Not after what just happened.

"Wa… meee?"

God almighty, what was he trying to say? The tequila bottle in his hand dropped to the floor, shattering as he reached for her. He hooked his arm around the back of her neck and smashed his lips to hers.

"Shit," Track hissed as we tried to pull Hero off Tara.

Tara brushed us away. "No. No, it's okay. I got him." She was a little taller than Madeline, but Hero was twice her size. No chance she could get him up to his bedroom on her own.

"Help her get him upstairs," I told Track. "If he gives you any trouble, Tara, get someone. My bedroom's at the end of the hall. Don't hesitate. He's not in his right mind. I'm not sure what he's capable of."

"We'll be fine, Storm. I can handle him." She wrapped her arms around his waist. "Come on, big guy."

"She wooves meee." Hero slurred his words.

I shook my head at Track as he helped Tara drag Hero out of the bar. "Make sure they're okay before you leave."

Madeline took my hand. "Where are they going?"

I hugged her, burying my face in her neck, inhaling her into my lungs. I hoped Tara could do for Hero what Madeline did for me.

"They're taking Hero to his room." I dropped a kiss on her lips. "Did you get any food yet?" I pressed my hand to her stomach, where my baby was safe inside her.

"No. I was waiting for you." She smiled so brightly I couldn't help but smile back.

"Angel, you know you don't have to wait for me. You need to eat so you can grow a healthy baby."

"I'll always wait for you. Forever."

CHAPTER TWENTY-EIGHT

MADELINE

My mom almost squeezed the air out of my body as she hugged me goodbye. It reminded me of when I'd go on tour with the church choir for a few weeks during my high school summers. She'd tell me to call and tell her goodnight the whole time I was gone. Said she needed to hear her baby's voice and to wish me sweet dreams. She had tried to hide it, but I knew she had tears rolling down her face every time.

I squeezed her back, trying to swallow down the emotion in my throat. "I love you, Mom. Thank you for coming." I should've made more of an effort calling her when I went off to college. Maybe if I had called her every night, I wouldn't have gotten together with Dane. But then, would I have met Storm?

"I love you too, sweetie. Keep in touch. I want to know how you and my grandbaby are doing." She kissed my head. "And Storm too." She pulled back, her blue eyes searching mine. "He loves you dearly."

I smiled, tearing up. "I love him dearly too." My chest got

those all too familiar flutters when I gazed over at my love. "He's incredible."

Storm winked at me while talking to my dad. God, he melted me.

"I can see that." She smiled. "I didn't want to ask in front of Storm, but do you think you'll get married?"

"Yes. When? I'm not sure. I guess after he proposes, we'll decide. Knowing him, he'd want to run off to elope."

Mom gasped, covering her mouth. She'd dreamed of my wedding since I was a little girl.

"Don't worry, I want a small wedding. Although, the whole club would probably be there."

She raised her brow. "Well, I hope they're on their best behavior."

"Storm will keep his brothers in line." I hoped he would, anyway. My parents were nice to everyone today, but that didn't mean people screwing in front of them was something they'd appreciate. Nor would I, at *my* wedding.

I suspected she wasn't thrilled about my new life and I couldn't blame her. Before Storm, I would have never considered getting involved with an outlaw biker. I was a law-abiding citizen. I'd thought dating a deputy was a good thing. Boy, was I wrong! Storm was a thousand percent a better man than Dane.

Stop. I forced thoughts of Dane from my mind.

"We should get on the road." Dad came up behind us and opened his arms to me. "Love you, sweetheart."

"Love you too, Dad."

He helped Mom into the car and shook Storm's hand. "Take care of my girl, son."

"Yes, sir. Drive safe." Storm tugged me into his arms after they got on the road. His hands rubbed my back, dipping low to my butt. "How are you doing?"

I wrapped my arms around his waist. "Good, all things considered."

It'd been a long, emotional day. All I wanted was to be with my protective, loving man.

"I'm ready to be alone with you." He swept me off my feet, cradling me in his arms. Could he hear my thoughts, the way he always knew what I wanted? Knowing Storm, probably. "How does that sound?"

I sighed dreamily, staring into his peaceful gaze. "Perfect."

"That's my girl."

The clubhouse was loud and rowdy as we passed the bar, heading for the stairs. A couple of his brothers made out hard and heavy, tucked into corners. My parents left in the nick of time. The usual naughty activities of the Knights were underway.

Storm jerked his chin at Lynx, who stopped at the staircase to let us go up first. Lynx had two kittens with him. The guy was rarely with one woman at a time.

Eminem blared through the speakers with "Not Afraid." My lungs burned and emotion bubbled in my chest. I tightened my grip around Storm's neck. AJ always seemed to be listening to Eminem while guarding me. I'd bet he was his favorite musician.

"Know what you're thinking about, Angel. I don't want you sad tonight, baby. Let's put AJ to rest."

I nodded, eyeing Hero's door. He and Tara hadn't shown their faces after she took him to his room. I assumed she was still with him. Couldn't hear anything as we passed.

Storm stopped at our door. "Grab my keys."

I reached my hand down into his pants pocket and fished out the key chain. I unlocked the door and locked it after Storm kicked it closed.

He set me on the edge of the bed. "How's my Angel *really* doing?" He knelt at my feet, removing my brown boots with the cross on the front. My aqua blue socks came off next.

"I'm okay, I guess." Twisting my lips because we both knew I was lying, I cradled his gorgeous face in my hands and kissed him.

I was uneasy knowing he was leaving on the run. I wasn't ready to be separated from him for a week. We'd only been apart once since we got together and that was the night before we discovered our real identities. Storm had assured me I would be safe with all the Hunters accounted for. Some were locked up in the county jail, and some were dead.

"Talk to me Angel," he said against my mouth.

"I'm terrified something will happen to you." *There, just tell him straight up.*

He pulled me into his embrace. "I won't lie to you, baby. These runs are always risky. It's not like it's a joy ride. If Hero was stable, I'd let him handle it with a crew of brothers. I can't take the chance right now. I wish that wasn't the case."

I knew it. My gut had been gnawing at me over this the last few days. "Dammit, Storm." I held onto him for dear life. "I can't lose you. I won't survive it."

"Yes, you will. If I don't make it back, you'll live on for our baby."

Tears filled my eyes as I reared back and shoved him hard in the chest. "Fuck you! You better come back to me. Don't talk like you might not. Don't." I hit his chest again. And again. Storm didn't budge. He flexed his solid wall of muscles, letting me beat out my frustrations. As my small fists hit his chest it was like he absorbed my fears. Slowly I calmed as his strength seeped into me. *I can do this… be strong for my man.*

"You know I won't lie to you. I will do everything possible to return, but I can't promise you I will."

I covered my face and cried, shaking my head. *So much for being strong.* I hated feeling emotionally unstable. Weak and vulnerable. Even if I had a good reason, it wasn't okay with me. I needed to be able to handle the MC life or Storm might decide I wasn't fit to be his old lady.

Stupid girl. You know he loves you. He'll never let you go. My insecurities were getting the better of me.

"Angel... Look at me." His deep voice soothed the ache in my chest. "I have something to ask you."

I sniffled, lowering my hands. "What?"

He presented the most beautiful, sparkling diamond solitaire ring. "Will you marry me?"

More tears streamed down my face but this time they were happy ones. I smiled, nodding into his devilishly handsome face, in awe— taken wholly by surprise when just seconds ago I was battling self-doubt.

In his typical, low-key form, there wasn't a big romantic speech. Nothing poetic. Just him on his knee, staring at me with those gorgeous stormy eyes, so full of love and admiration—and a cocky curl on his tempting lips.

"Is that even a question?" My heart sang as he slid the ring onto my finger. My childhood crush just asked me to marry him. Dreams really did come true.

"Gimme the words, Angel. I need to hear them."

I dropped onto his lap, throwing my arms around his neck. "Yes, Kaleb, I will marry you." Everything we were talking about before this moment faded away as our lips connected.

Storm raised to his feet with me in his arms and put me on the bed, breaking our liplock. Without a single word, his heated gaze seared my skin like he was about to ravage me. He was so damn sexy as he removed his clothes—broad chest and corded muscles everywhere. I eyed the club's patch tattooed on his bicep. There was nothing sexier than this fierce man... the president of a motorcycle club, who loved me. Me.

I was his world just as he was mine.

"You gonna leave that dress on, or do I need to rip it off your luscious body?"

I shivered at his warning tone. He turned me on every minute of every day with his deep, husky voice. Climbing onto my knees before him, I smiled mischievously. "Do what you need to do."

His eyebrows raised. "I'll buy you a new dress." At the neckline, he ripped the fabric all the way down to the hem. The sound made my skin prickle with excitement. Storm tossed my shredded garment aside, and his hot hands were on me. His fingers glided over my legs, torso, and breasts, teasing and driving me wild with the lightest of touches.

I sighed, giving myself over to him. "I love you," I told him, gripping his large shoulders and dropping my head back.

He kissed my stomach. "Love you too, Angel. Love you both." He unhooked my bra and licked my nipples, showing both equal attention. I almost collapsed from the sensations spiraling through my body. My nipples had been super sensitive, even painful at times, when he sucked on them. It enhanced our lovemaking—that sting of pain propelling me into deeper levels of climax.

Storm gazed into my eyes, lowering me to the sheets. "I want to get married right away. As soon as I get back from the run."

I flashed a face-splitting grin. "I'd love that. But I'll need a few weeks to put something together."

"Sugar and Tina can help. Whatever you want or need, it's yours. All I want is to be your husband as soon as possible."

Jesus, he nearly made me weep the way he loved me so completely. "I want the same, baby."

He settled between my legs, entering me. We groaned as I hooked my legs around the backs of his thighs, taking him in deeper. He lowered his mouth to mine, inhaling me into his lungs with each lash of his tongue. This was my favorite place to be, under his massive body, with his huge, thick cock inside. Feeling his heart beat in time with mine, connected body and soul.

This was my heaven—both of us surrendering to each other.

Storm drew his cock out until only the tip graced my opening, then thrust back inside, going balls deep. He repeated this air stealing move, making love to me while we kissed.

Lifting us both into the clouds, he increased his tempo until we shot off together.

I clawed at his back as he dug his fingers into my hips, holding me just where he wanted me. He released my lips, dropping his forehead to mine, panting.

"You're everything to me, Angel. Everything." His head lifted and his platinum eyes shimmered with unshed tears. "Goddamn, I love you so much it hurts.

I played with the base of his neck the way he liked. Emotion bubbling into my throat. "You're coming back to me, right?"

"Not even the Reaper could stop me." He dropped a kiss on my lips, then slipped out of me.

After cleaning us both, Storm took me into his arms, holding my head against his heart. His fingers skated over the tattoo just below my neck... his mark. "Let's get some sleep."

I wouldn't ask him to promise to come back because he wouldn't be able to give me the words I wanted to hear. Still, in my heart, I knew he'd return. There was no earthly force strong enough to stop my all-powerful Storm. Nothing and no one could keep my fierce man from his baby and me.

I took comfort in that.

EPILOGUE

STORM

I squeezed my Angel as we swayed to the music in the middle of the dance floor at The Bullet. Our wedding ceremony had been short and sweet, just how we wanted. The trees in the backyard of the clubhouse were in various fall colors, the air crisp. It was perfect with flowers decorating the gazebo I'd bought for my girl back in August. I loved that we said our vows in it. Madeline's friend, Ray, sang a song I'd never heard before. It didn't even matter, the damn thing made me tear up as I stared at my beauty. I wasn't a mushy guy, far from it, but I'd been a little emotional soaring in the clouds all fuckin' day, crazy happy.

Madeline had wanted to have our reception in the place we'd seen each other for the first time after I'd left Garrison. I thought it was a terrific idea, so I closed the bar for our celebration. Everyone was here, all my brothers, Angel's teacher friends, and both of our families. Even Toby made it out.

A month had passed since I returned from the arms run up to

Canada. The delivery had been uneventful, to my relief. However, Hero, my Sergeant at Arms, hadn't been doing so great. We were halfway home when my brother pulled me over on the side of the highway to tell me he needed to go deal with his demons and wasn't returning Bastion with the rest of us.

I could've forced Hero, but it wouldn't have done any good. I knew what it was like to live with guilt. It tormented the mind and ate at you from the inside out.

Hero hadn't been the same since the Hunters took him and the girls. I'd thought he was doing better after he let Tara take care of him the night of AJ's memorial. They'd stayed holed up in his room until the morning we left on the run.

I really thought he was in a better headspace when I'd heard him say, "Roja, stay in my room. Move your shit to the clubhouse."

I'd just finished kissing my woman and straddled my bike. But then, I noticed he wasn't okay.

Tara had gone to kiss Hero, but he'd gripped her wrists and pushed her away. From there, it got all dramatic and shit. Tara started to cry. Madeline had turned to me for answers I didn't have for her.

I thought Hero might've been back for the wedding. He'd checked in—just like I made him promise—but no dice. Hero was hellbent on fighting his demons.

And Tara?

She'd been depressed ever since we left on the run. When I returned without Hero, the redhead shut down. Madeline and I were both worried, but two weeks later, Tara acted as if nothing happened. She flipped a one-eighty and moved her shit out of Hero's room. I couldn't let her leave in good conscience, after Hero demanded she stayed in his room. Eventually, with Madeline's help, we convinced Tara to stay in one of our basement dorms.

I still felt the loss of Hero, though. He was one of my closest friends, my SAA. Now that he wasn't here, Track had taken up the slack.

"Are you happy, Angel?" I kissed her head. She looked breathtakingly gorgeous in her ivory lace dress and those fuckin' sexy brown boots with the cross on the front. She called it a high-low wedding dress with a sweetheart neckline. Had no idea what she meant, nor did I ask for her to explain it. To me, it was beautiful and perfect on her. And I loved seeing her wearing my favorite boots. Even better were her plump tits popping out the top of her "sweetheart neckline." I couldn't wait to get her home to ravage her.

"Exceedingly happy. You?" She peered up at me, a radiant smile on her lovely face.

"That's all I want, Angel. For you to be happy." I spun her around, doing my best to be everything she wanted during our wedding dance. She'd picked some country song I didn't know, said it was her favorite and made her think of me. Damn, she was the sweetest thing. She'd been singing the whole time. Belting out the lyrics and melting me with her fuckin' incredible voice. She seriously needed to consider performing more often, maybe starting her own band. But I knew it wasn't what she wanted.

"What song is this?" I asked against her ear.

"It's "Speechless" by Dan and Shay." She smiled.

"Speechless, huh?" I certainly was as I held my wife in my arms. *My wife*. I couldn't be more blissed-out in love with her.

One final spin for dramatics and I dipped her, sealing my lips to hers.

The room filled with whistling and cheering as Madeline giggled against my lips. I loved seeing her this way. Relaxed and serene, and deliriously in love with me. She didn't have to worry about anything or anyone. All the threats had been eliminated.

Well, Deputy fuckin' Miller hadn't met his maker yet, but he would soon. I just needed to bide my time a bit longer before I took that prick out.

Madeline ended our kiss. "You're my wildest dream come true."

"Angel, I'm the luckiest fucker on the planet."

She tossed her head back, giggling, and I helped myself to a taste of her neck. We stayed there, not caring we were the center of everyone's attention.

An eerie silence descended on the bar and I reeled Madeline in closer to my body.

"Storm, my dad is here." Sugar tapped my arm.

"Shit." I lifted Madeline back up. She took my hand, lacing our fingers. "Baby, stay with Sugar." I kissed her hand as I cut my gaze to Sheriff Hendricks. The grim expression on his face made my gut twist.

Sugar put her arm around Madeline just as Tara joined them.

I nodded. "Sheriff."

Raul, Track, and Boxer appeared next to me.

"Storm. Sorry to interrupt your celebration." He dragged his hand across his face, glancing around the room at all the onlookers.

"What is it?" I fisted my hands, bracing myself for what he was about to say. This was bad. Felt it in my bones. Jim wouldn't have come here if it wasn't necessary. He knew today was my wedding. He'd been at the small ceremony earlier on the compound.

"Hero's down in county lockup."

Are you curious about what kind of trouble Hero got himself into?
Find out in **HELLBENT HERO**!

Do you want to talk about Storm and his brothers? Or maybe you want the inside scoop on KLMC? Join *Naomi's Knight's Legion MC,* a private reader group on Facebook!

ALSO BY NAOMI PORTER

St. James Billionaires

Breach of Honor (Part one of duet)
Bound by Love (Part two of duet)
Blinded by Loyalty
Battle of Wills (Releasing early fall 2021)

Bad Boys We Love

Neighbor Nik
Lifeguard Leo
Effing Eli
Fireman Fox

ACKNOWLEDGEMENT

First and foremost, to my super supportive husband and kids. I wouldn't be where I am without your patience. Thank you, thank you, thank you!

To my freaking fantastic editor, Marissa Gramoll, I love working with you! Reading your comments was the highlight of my day. Thank you for loving my characters and making their story shine.

To my proofreader, Beth at Magnolia Author Services, thank you for polishing my books. I appreciated your efficiency and professionalism.

To my author friend and fellow MC author, Stevie Lee. Thank you for commenting on that Facebook post. Your friendship and support have meant a lot to me. You are a treasure! XO

To my dear author friend, Sarah Bailey. I feel like we've been on our writing journey together every step of the way. I couldn't have asked for a better person to share this incredible experience with. You've gotten me through some rough moments and made me cry-laughing many other times. Thank you for always being there for me. I love you, friend!

All the love,

Naomi

ABOUT THE AUTHOR

Naomi Porter always had a knack for storytelling, and she's finally putting pen to paper to share with you, the reader. Whether she's trying to stay warm during freezing winter weather or cool in the sweltering heat, she's pounding away at the keys of her laptop to bring you the latest gritty motorcycle club romance, decadent billionaire saga, or heart-stopping sexy drama.

No matter what story she's telling, you can bet it has sexy as sin men, sassy and confident women, and plenty of sizzling passion.